BLOOD AND SAND

A JOHN JORDAN MYSTERY THRILLER BOOK 23

MICHAEL LISTER

PULPWOOD PRESS

Hardback ISBN: 978-1-947606-52-4

Paperback ISBN: 978-1-947606-51-7

Books by Michael Lister

(John Jordan Novels)
Power in the Blood
Blood of the Lamb
Flesh and Blood
(Special Introduction by Margaret Coel)
The Body and the Blood
Double Exposure
Blood Sacrifice
Rivers to Blood
Burnt Offerings
Innocent Blood
(Special Introduction by Michael Connelly)
Separation Anxiety
Blood Money
Blood Moon
Thunder Beach
Blood Cries
A Certain Retribution
Blood Oath
Blood Work
Cold Blood

Blood Betrayal
Blood Shot
Blood Ties
Blood Stone
Blood Trail
Bloodshed
Blue Blood
And the Sea Became Blood
The Blood-Dimmed Tide
Blood and Sand
A John Jordan Christmas

(Jimmy Riley Novels)
The Girl Who Said Goodbye
The Girl in the Grave
The Girl at the End of the Long Dark Night
The Girl Who Cried Blood Tears
The Girl Who Blew Up the World

(Merrick McKnight / Reggie Summers Novels)
Thunder Beach
A Certain Retribution
Blood Oath
Blood Shot

(Remington James Novels)
Double Exposure
(includes intro by Michael Connelly)
Separation Anxiety
Blood Shot

(Sam Michaels / Daniel Davis Novels)
Burnt Offerings
Blood Oath
Cold Blood
Blood Shot

(Love Stories)
Carrie's Gift

For all the children who don't come home and the parents still waiting for them.

THANK YOU!

Dawn Lister, Aaron Bearden, Jill Mueller, Tim Flanagan, and Dr, D.P. Lyle.

Thanks for all your invaluable contributions!

BLOOD AND SAND

DAY 3

Day 3

My little Magdalene has been missing for three days. Every second that ticks by, it becomes less and less likely that we'll ever get her back.

My friend Henrique, a retired journalist who runs our little newspaper here, suggested I start a journal. He knows I'm losing my mind and thinks writing down some of my thoughts and feelings will be therapeutic. Maybe it will be. He says writing about things has always helped him, though I doubt he's ever had to write about anything like this.

I still can't believe my little Magdalene is gone. I keep expecting to wake up and realize that she's here and that the whole thing was a nightmare. Or I think one of the searchers will walk in with her at any moment and tell us everything's okay, that she had just gotten lost. But I know neither one of those scenarios is possible. She didn't just wander off somehow. She couldn't even get out of our house on her own. And a three-year-old can't survive on her own for three days. I know this is all real. All too real.

I keep thinking about that perfect day we had just a few weeks ago—just me, Keith, and Magdalene on an empty beach in the late afternoon. Seems like a dream now, like something that I observed instead of experienced. But it's so vivid, so detailed in every way. I can still feel the sun on my face, hear the wind in my ears—the wind and Magdalene's squeals and shrieks and laughter. I can see her sun-kissed hair waving in the breeze and that contented, happy look on her sweet little face.

What was the last thing I said to her? I can't remember now. What must she be thinking? Going through? How must she feel? Terrified. Confused. Is she wondering why we don't come get her? Does she think we abandoned her? Does she know how loved she is? Is she even still alive to be able to have such thoughts and feelings?

I don't know many of the details about how difficult her life was before she went into foster care, but whatever situation she's in now has to be far worse than anything she's ever experienced before. It doubly breaks my heart and makes me want to kill myself when I think of some of the darker possibilities of what might be happening to her.

I just want to hold her. I just want to hug her. I just want to read her a story. I just want to tell her how much I love her again and again and again and again and again and again and again. I just want her with me. I never want her to leave my side again, not for the rest of her life.

I've read enough true crime and watched enough crime shows to know that every hour that passes means it's less likely that we will ever find her. For three days to have already passed fills me with such hopelessness I'm finding it hard to function.

I can't understand why the whole world won't just stop and help us find her. How can people go on with their lives like everything is okay?

Someone just reminded me it's Christmas. Would've been our first Christmas together, but instead all my little girl's gifts are unopened under the tree.

1

The mid-morning sun is high and bright, its warmth present in the sand beneath our bare feet and seen in the shimmer on the calm surface of the Gulf of Mexico's green waters.

Though Taylor's little white dress comes to just below her knees and my suit pants are rolled up, tiny particles of the sun-heated sand still cling to our clothes.

It's a Sunday morning in early November, a little less than a month removed from the destruction and devastation of Hurricane Michael, the category 5 superstorm that ripped through the region where our roots are still firmly planted.

The only noticeable nod to autumn is the decreased humidity in the currents of coastal air swirling around us.

We are in the little, unincorporated master-planned community of Sandcastle on 30A—one of many high-end vacation destinations for wealthy families lining the scenic route that runs parallel to Highway 98 between Panama City Beach and Destin. Of the many beach-chic master-planned communities located here—Rosemary, Alys, WaterColor, Grayton—by far the most popular and famous is Seaside, not only because it was one of the first in the country to be designed using the principles of new urbanism, but because Peter Weir's *The Truman Show* was filmed here.

Before us the Gulf looks like green glass, beneath us the sand is like sugar, behind us the quaint little town appears to be a pastel postcard. The weather is perfect. The beach is pristine. The town is picturesque. This idyllic setting makes it nearly impossible to imagine that a three-year-old little girl could vanish from here and never be seen again. It also makes it difficult to fathom that less than sixty miles away, my part of the panhandle is a post-apocalyptic wasteland.

Just thinking about the condition I left it in floods my mind with dread and fills my heart with guilt.

The New Florida communities along 30A have always seemed a world apart from their rural and impoverished Old Florida neighbors of Wewahitchka, Panama City, and Pottersville, but Hurricane Michael has elevated that to an unimaginable new extreme.

We are here because I've been invited to give a series of talks in the town's nonsectarian chapel this week—for which we are getting a family vacation we couldn't otherwise afford.

When I had originally accepted the invitation to give the lecture series and stay here with my family, I did so in hopes of looking into the disappearance of Magdalene Dacosta, but that was before the hurricane and my wrongful death trial—and Anna's strange behavior, including her ongoing insistence that I stop my extracurricular investigations.

My first talk begins in just a few minutes, but when we arrived a few minutes ago and Taylor asked if we could take a quick walk on the beach, I couldn't say no.

I couldn't say no, but Anna, my wife and Taylor's mom, could, which is why she is waiting for us in protest in the car. She had used the excuse of wanting to hear the end of a public radio report we had been listening to on the drive over—one about a new barter economy in certain developing nations where illegally harvested organs and even kidnapped children are being traded for medical treatment by Americans with means. But we both know the real reason she refused to join us.

It's one of many out-of-character actions she's taken recently that have me concerned both for her and our relationship.

Perhaps it's a result of the residual effects from the hurricane, the lingering, often subconscious trauma of the unprecedented storm and its unmooring aftermath, or maybe it's the added stress of having to defend me in a wrongful death case, or perhaps it's the fatigue of being a working wife and mother of small children, or maybe it really is just me. Whatever it is—a combination of some or all of these or something that hasn't even occurred to me yet—my wife and closest confidant has changed, at least in how she relates to me. And so far I have yet to be able to figure out the exact reasons for it or what I might be able to do about it.

None of our family or friends have noticed any of this. The ever-so-slight change in Anna is so subtle as to be nearly imperceptible. She has said very little and nothing directly, and when I ask her about her behavior, even press her on it, she acts as if she doesn't know what I'm talking about. But it's there—mostly in the form of a faint formality, a nearly indiscernible distance, a vagueness and indeterminate distraction.

I'm hoping that this much-needed week of rest and relaxation and time away from our stressful and depressing post-storm reality will address at least two of her most often expressed complaints—that I work too much and that I don't have the relationship she wants me to with Taylor. Her expressions of these grievances are most often nonverbal and easily deniable—a momentary altering of her breathing or a flicker of a facial expression or an almost imperceptible pulling back of her presence.

One week at the beach isn't going to fix anything, but it should at least create some opportunities for us to actually discuss whatever's going on and for me to begin to make adjustments, for us to take the first steps toward an ongoing repairing and reprogramming. It could be where we hit reset and restart.

Anna's actual dissatisfaction isn't that I work too much and that I don't have the relationship she wants me to with Taylor, but that I never stop working, never put my mind in neutral, and that I don't have the relationship with Taylor that I have with my daughter Johanna.

But there's more to it than just that, because here we are on vacation and here I am spending time with Taylor doing what Taylor wants to do—and Anna still appears dissatisfied and seems ever so slightly distant.

"I need to go over to the chapel now," I say to Taylor. "It's almost time for my talk."

She nods but the disappointment shows on her four-year-old face.

"We'll come back this afternoon," I say. "And we'll be here all week, so we can play on the beach every day."

She nods again and lifts her small hand up for me to take so I can help her negotiate the softer sand between us and the car.

"Wish Mama would'a come down with us," she says, her face down to ensure she doesn't step on the sharp edge of a shell or a sea or sand critter of some kind.

"Me too. Maybe this afternoon. And Johanna will be here in a few days."

"*Yay,*" she says in the way only an adoring little sister can.

As Taylor and I walk hand in hand toward Anna, who is now out of and leaning against the parked car, I have a momentary flash of something familiar that feels like an instant of déjà vu.

I recall a recurring dream I've had over the years.

·   ·   ·

THE LAST OF the setting sun streaks the blue horizon with neon pink and splatters the emerald green waters of the Gulf with giant orange splotches like scoops of sherbet in an art deco bowl.

A fitting finale for a perfect Florida day.

My son, who looks to be around four, though it's hard to tell since in dreams we all seem ageless—runs up from the water's edge, his face red with sun and heat, his hands sticky with wet sand, and asks me to join him for one last swim.

He looks up at me with his mother's brown eyes, as open and honest as possible, and smiles his sweetest smile as he begins to beg.

"Please, Daddy," he says. "Please."

"We need to go," I say. "It'll be dark soon. And I'm supposed to take your mom out on a date tonight."

"Please, Daddy," he repeats as if I have not spoken, and now he takes the edge of my swimming trunks in his tiny, sandy hand and tugs.

I look down at him, moved by his openness, purity, and beauty.

He knows he's got me then.

"Yes," he says, releasing my shorts to clench his fist and pull it toward him in a gesture of victory. Then he begins to jump up and down.

I drop the keys and the towels and the bottles of sunscreen wrapped in them, kick off my flip-flops, and pause just a moment to take it all in—him, the sand, the sea, the sun.

"I love you, Dad," he says with the ease and unashamed openness only a safe and secure child can.

"I love you."

I take his hand in mine, and we walk down to the end of his world as the sun sets and the breeze cools off the day. And we walk right into the ocean from which we came. A wave knocks us down and we stay that way, allowing the foamy water to wash over us.

He shrieks his joy and excitement, sounding like the gulls in the air and on the shore. He plays with intensity and abandon, and for a *moment I want to be a child again—but only for a moment, for more than anything in this world, I want to be his dad.*

We forget about the world around us, and we lose track of time, and the thick, salty waters of the Gulf roll in on us and then back out to sea.

I FIRST HAD the dream when Susan and I had been working on reconciling, and at the time, I thought it was about a son we would have together one day. When Susan and I split up and I was single again I'd occasionally have the dream. I then believed it to be about a son I'd have in the future with a yet to be determined woman I had hoped would be Anna.

When later I discovered that Susan and I had a little girl, I had believed the dream was about our little Johanna and that the gender of the child in the dream was irrelevant.

But then I continued to have the dream.

Many people, including experts on dreams, believe that recurring dreams are a sign of something unresolved—an unaddressed stress or an unacknowledged childhood trauma—but my experience of this particular repeating dream has never felt like any of that.

The dream resurfaced later when it looked as if Anna and I were going to adopt Carla's son John Paul, and I believed it had been about him all along. But then when Carla decided to keep him, I again had no idea what it meant.

Maybe the dream isn't about a literal son or child at all. Maybe it has a symbolic meaning I've yet to discern. Whatever it is remains a mystery—one made all the more mysterious and relevant by its recurring nature.

Whether arising from my thoughts about the subtle changes I've noticed in Anna or the experience of déjà vu and the recurring nature of the dream that caused it, I find that in spite of the pleasant morning and the pleasurable moment

Taylor and I have just shared in this peaceful, picturesque place, I am filled with an acute sense of apprehension.

Day 4

I honestly don't know how we're doing it.

I mean how we're functioning at all.

We are functioning, I guess—at least somewhat—and that seems impossible.

How are we actually waking up each morning? How are we getting out of bed? (To be fair, sometimes I don't.) How are we getting ready and getting dressed? How are we putting one foot in front of the other? How are we still living?

It must be that we don't know where Magdalene is and what happened to her. If we knew for sure she wasn't coming home to us . . . I mean we know, but we don't know-know—not like for absolute certain. If I did—if I knew for absolute certain that she was never coming home to us again, I don't think I'd get up. Not in the morning. Not ever again. Keith might be able to— probably would—but not me. I couldn't.

I'm so numb it's like I'm not really alive.

I've never felt this dull before, this dead.

You would think feeling nothing would really feel like not feeling at all, but that's not how it is. Feeling nothing actually has a feeling. A lack of feeling is a feeling. It's sort of like the sound of silence. Silence does have a sound. It can be deafening. And feeling nothing can be excruciating.

DAY 5

Day 5

The Florida House has become the Forensic House. Our beloved dream home and B&B will forever be marred. Forensics is finished with our house, but I'm not sure I can ever stay here again. It certainly will never be a home again—not unless we get Magdalene back and can be a family again. But even then, would I want to live somewhere where she had been taken from? I don't think I could. But even if I could, I couldn't do that to her. I used to love our home. This house is very special. Or was. A unique, one-of-a-kind labyrinth of love. And it has always been such an expression of who we are. The architecture and construction, the secret passageways and hidden rooms, a reflection of Keith. The furniture and decorations, the comfort and coziness, a reflection of me.

It was our dream home. Now it's our nightmare house of horrors.

For now, no matter what else we decide to do, I'm keeping Magdalene's room just the way it is for as long as we live here. No matter what. The only thing I'm going to do is take her unopened Christmas presents from under the tree and put them in her room. Everything else will stay just as it was. Well, just as it is now that the crime scene unit is finished with it.

I'm still hoping we'll get Magdalene back soon and she can open her presents. We'll put Christmas on hold until she comes home—no matter how long that is. And if she never comes home again, then I will never celebrate Christmas again.

2

The assigned topic of my talk today is The State of the World and What to Do about It. Following each talk there will be a talkback where attendees get to respond to what I say with comments and questions.

"This is a big topic," I say. "Not one I feel qualified to address. In some ways the state of the world is obvious, but what to do about it . . . there's a question. I think in one sense the state of the world is as it ever was, but in another it's—at least in ways—a whole new world."

I am a bit preoccupied by what appears to be Anna's lack of engagement. It's subtle—something maybe no one else would notice—but compared to her usual eye contact and encouraging nods and sweet smiles, she seems disinterested and distracted.

"It seems to me that human history is the narrative of human nature—of the continual conflict between our default settings of selfishness and self-centeredness and the better angels of our natures. At our worst we are tribal and brutal—and we're seeing plenty of examples of this. Rampant xenophobia and the demonization of the *other*, the different. Bold and blatant abuse of those not *us*, who are seen to pose a threat to *us*. We hear it in the rhetoric and see it in the actions of many among us."

I don't speak for long—less than fifteen minutes. How to Save the World in a Quarter Hour. I can't remember everything I say, but it's mostly a brief introduction for the discussion to follow and the later sessions throughout the week.

"I don't have the answers, the solutions to resolve the world's enormous issues," I say, "but I know it all comes down to love. Ever-expanding love that leads to equality and unselfishness, that treats the *other* not as an *other* at all—but as, like the Austrian philosopher Martin Buber said, a *thou* instead of an *it*. We don't treat others inhumanely unless we see them as less than human—less human than us. Be they immigrants or minorities or women or a different religion, culture, political party, or sexual orientation from us, it's only when we view them as less than that we treat them as less than. Humanity is hardwired to be tribal. We care for and protect and connect with and share with and believe the best about those in our tribe. So what love does is increase our compassion and understanding to such an extent that eventually and ultimately it places everyone—all the people on the planet—in our tribe. Of course, this won't end conflicts or problems, but it seems to me that there's no question that we handle these issues far differently with people inside our tribe than for those without."

The gathered group is a mixture of permanent residents, those who work on 30A but can't afford to live here, and the wealthy of Atlanta, Nashville, and Birmingham vacationing here.

Though not very diverse racially, they are one of the most socioeconomically diverse groups I've spoken to in quite some time. Seated on the same pews are the old-moneyed wealthy who manage millions and the seasonal barely-above-minimum-wage working poor who manage somehow to make it even though they don't earn a living wage. It will be interesting to see the extent to which this diversity shows up in the questions and comments during the talkback.

I enjoy sharing my few brief thoughts with the audience. It has been a while since I've spoken to a congregation—well, a while for someone who's accustomed to doing it weekly. I haven't had a congregation of my own since Hurricane Michael decimated much of Gulf Correctional Institution where I was chaplain and the inmates had to be shipped off to other facilities around the state.

Because of the hurricane's destruction and the uncertainty around when exactly the prison's reconstruction will be completed, and because I was unwilling to move even temporarily to work at a different facility, I resigned. For the first time in a long time I have only one job—that of investigator with the Gulf County Sheriff's Department, and I'm hoping for more opportunities like this one to give inspirational talks at various places or to fill in for ministers away in training or on vacation. Of course, such opportunities and invitations will probably be determined by how this week goes, which based on the first question is not promising.

"Are you really saying *all we need is love*?"

The questioner, a sixty-something white man with a halo of sparse, wool-like hair and a perpetual scowl above the half-glasses permanently poised on the end of his nose, can't hide the disdain from his voice. Of course, it's highly likely he doesn't try.

"Not in a pop song kind of way," I say. "Not in a trite, sentimental, theoretical way, no. But in the 'fighting against our selfish natures in order to extend ourselves on the behalf of others' way, 'to put ourselves in their place and to care for them as we care for ourselves' way, yes."

"How'd that work out for the hippies?" he says.

"It works well for everyone who truly practices it."

"I guess you and I—and Jesus come to that—have differing notions of what *working out well* means."

"I dare say we do," I say, nodding and smiling.

"Smile insipidly if you want to," he says, "but 'Kumbaya' around the campfire won't solve anything, let alone everything."

"On that we agree completely."

DAY 11

Day 11

I don't want to eat or sleep or do anything but look for Magdalene.

If even a moment passes by when I'm not thinking about her or trying to find her, I feel more guilt than I ever have about anything in my entire life.

I was shocked when Keith wanted to make love last night. How can he even think about anything pleasurable or enjoyable while our little girl is out there somewhere with God only knows what being done to her? I didn't handle it well. I didn't mean to come across as so harsh and judgmental, but I really was just floored that he could even want to. He said it would be healing and restorative and help us be closer and have the wherewithal to go on, but I just couldn't. I can't.

Keith is being so patient with me, so good to me. I know he feels so guilty about that night. And as much as it hurts me to think it, he should. But it's causing him to be even more attentive and patient. Ordinarily he would've gotten mad about the way I acted and the things I said. And that would be on top of his frustration from not having sex. But he didn't get upset or offended or anything. He just apologized and held me. It was sweet.

3

W e have lunch in the dining room of the Florida
House—the bed and breakfast we're staying in
this week.

The dining room is larger than those found in most homes,
but not by much. A long, wide wooden table that seats ten
leaves little space for anything else. Twelve people, counting
Taylor who sits on an end corner between me and Anna, are
crowded around the table.

Our hosts and the owners of the B&B, Keith and Christopher Dacosta, sit at the opposite end of the table from us. They
are gracious, warm, and welcoming, but each of them wears a
subtle but palpable shroud of sadness.

In their early to mid-thirties, the two men are trim and stylish, though in different ways. Keith is more muscular and
dressed more casually, and Christopher is slighter, softer, and
more soft-spoken.

Between them and us the table is filled with many of the
movers and shakers of Sandcastle.

There's Wren Melody, the tall, thin, short-haired British
lady of older but indeterminate age—is she fifty-five or seventy-

five?—who owns the bookshop. Brooke Wakefield, the twenty-something painstakingly put together platinum blonde who operates the boutique. Clarence and Sarah Samuelson, the forty-something couple who run the restaurant. Vic Frankford, the middle-aged man who owns the grocery store. Rake Sabin, the proprietor of the bicycle rental place, Wheel of Time. And Henrique Arango, the fifty-something Cuban gentleman who serves as editor of the newspaper.

"A very inspiring talk, dear boy," Wren Melody says. Her British accent is faint but still present. "Most rousing. Looking forward to the others still to come."

"Thank you," I say.

"Inspirational, yes," Vic Frankford says, his short, coarse salt-and-pepper hair not moving as he first nods then shakes his head. "Realistic, no. And maybe even dangerous." His hands are thick, his nails manicured, and he wears a pinky ring on his right hand. His easy, smooth, confident nonchalance gives him the feel of being a made man.

"How so?" Henrique Arango asks, his dark eyes widening above their dark circles, his expression pushing his glasses up his nose.

"Aspirations of utopia are as dangerously hopeful as dread of dystopia are dangerously despairing."

I shake my head. "I'm sorry if I wasn't clear," I say. "I was in no way describing a utopia. I well know the dangers of believing in the *deus ex machina* of humanity evolving en masse into something akin to perfection. It's as hollow as the belief that a literal god in the machine will pull back the curtain, stop human history, and make everything right and new. No, what I was speaking to was what we as individuals can do. We can't change anyone else or make anyone else do anything—except temporarily by the immoral means of force or manipulation. We can only change ourselves. We are only responsible for ourselves. I was only speaking to what is the best way to live for us individually. And of course that determines how we spend our time and money and how we vote and what causes we support. If everyone is in our tribe, then we're not going to do business with those who treat another group as less than and in supposed need of conversion or marginalization or eradication. We're not going to vote for or support any candidate or party or administration that is nationalistic, racist, xenophobic, or even uses any rhetoric a neo-Nazi could find the least bit of solidarity with. But that's all secondary to how we live, what we say and do—in our private, unguarded, and unobserved moments and in our more public words and actions."

"It's not easy, though, is it?" Christopher Dacosta says.

He's staring off into the distance and doesn't seem to be speaking to any of us. His diminutive size, pale, unlined, clean-shaven face, and soft-spoken voice give him a boyish quality not often found in men his age.

Keith puts his hand on his back and pats and rubs him.

"How can you love or allow into your tribe those who are evil?" Christopher asks. "Predators who prey on innocence and the jackals who rush in afterward to pick the bones clean?"

Seeming far more like an inward musing that wasn't meant to be verbalized than an actual question directed toward me, I don't respond, just continue to listen.

The entire tone and temperature of the room changes, and everyone at the table stops—stops talking, eating, moving, even breathing for a moment.

Anna looks over at me, her quizzical expression asking if I know what he's referring to, and though I do, I don't let on that I do.

Last year, just three days before Christmas, Keith and Christopher's three-year-old adopted daughter, Magdalene, went missing and hasn't been seen since. As is the pattern in most of the cases like theirs, Keith and Christopher went from sympathized-with victims to villainized-and-demonized suspects faster than you can say *John and Patsy Ramsey and Kate and Gerry McCann.*

I'm assuming the predator Christopher is speaking of is the perpetrator who abducted Magdalene, and the jackals who pick the bones clean afterward are the press and the public who turned on her grieving parents.

"I don't know," I say. "Maybe it's not possible. I don't believe I can tell anyone else what they should do, but especially not those who have suffered beyond my ability to even comprehend. And I believe in attempting to get justice, in imprisoning predators so they can never again repeat their unimaginable atrocities. But . . . I am convinced by and believe in the absolute healing power of love and the ability of forgiveness to free us from the self-imposed prison cell that hate relegates us to."

DAY 13

Day 13

There are only a few reasons why anyone would abduct a child, and none of them are good.

I just keep thinking about what might be happening to my sweet little girl. Or, if she's already dead, what might have happened to her before she was killed.

It's absolute torture. It's driving me mad. These images keep flashing in my imagination. They're horrific beyond anything I've ever even heard about and I keep seeing them happen to my Magdalene.

I say it's torture, but it's nothing compared to what Magdalene has likely been through.

I want to jab a long knife into my ear or an icepick into my eye to get the images out of my head.

Please, God, make it stop. Please forgive me if I ever did anything to deserve this. I'm sorry. I repent. I take it back. Please.

Unless . . . Don't stop it if Magdalene is still suffering. I want to suffer as long as she does. Let me suffer instead of her. Heap it on me. I can take it. Just spare her.

4

"We really appreciate what you shared today," Keith is saying. "It was a great talk and we look forward to your others, but . . ."

After lunch, Keith and Christopher had asked to speak to me in private.

We are in the small kitchen in the back part of their B&B that serves as their primary residence.

"Well, we . . ." Keith continues. "The main reason we were so eager to have you speak at chapel this week and to stay here in our home is because we'd really like you to look into Magdalene's case for us."

"We've heard about you from a few different people we trust," Christopher says. "We read about some of the cases you worked on and listened to a few true crime podcasts about others."

"The truth is," Keith says, "the reporter who has been the fairest to us, who seems to be an actual decent human being, Merrick McKnight, said if anyone could figure out what really happened to Magdalene, you could."

They're telling me that one of the main reasons they asked

me to come speak is they hoped I'd look into Magdalene's disappearance. But what I can't tell them—especially because of how strained my relationship with Anna is right now over this very thing—is that a big part of the reason I accepted the invitation is that I was hoping to get a chance to look into Magdalene's disappearance for myself. In addition to welcoming the chance to speak on the topics selected and getting away from our hurricane-ravaged hometown for a much-needed family vacation, of course."We made you this," Christopher says, handing me a large binder that looks like a homemade murder book.

I take the binder, touching the photograph of Magdalene glued to the front of it, then open it and begin to flip through its carefully constructed pages.

"It's got everything we've been able to get our hands on," Keith adds. "Statements, interviews, evidence, theories, articles, suspects, everything—even Chris's journal. There's a lot the police won't give us, but we're hoping maybe you could get that."

It's entirely possible the authorities don't have nearly as much as he thinks.

"This is impressive," I say.

Keith says, "Chris is a scrapbooker."

In the short time I've been here, I've noticed that Keith is the only one permitted to call Christopher *Chris*.

"I'm so, so sorry that she was taken," I say.

"Thank you," Christopher says.

"Will you look into it for us?" Keith asks.

"I'd really like to," I say.

"*But*?" Keith asks.

"There's no *but* like that," I say. "Just a few caveats and explanations."

"Okay," he says. "Let's hear them."

"I take very seriously the talks I'm giving," I say. "And part of the reason I'm here is to enjoy a little vacation time with my family. I won't short shrift either of them."

"Understood," Keith says.

"I hope the talks weren't just an excuse to get me here to talk to me about—"

"Absolutely not," Christopher says. "You were chosen by a committee. We only got one vote like everybody else. It was an enthusiastic vote, but we were just two of eight."

"And we weren't even the ones who recommended you in the first place," Keith says.

I nod, then continue. "If I start this, I won't stop until it's solved to my satisfaction. I'm still investigating some of the Atlanta Child Murders from forty years ago."

"That's what we want," Christopher says. "I mean, we hope it doesn't take that long, of course, but we wouldn't want you to stop until it's over."

"I will follow the evidence where it leads," I say. "I don't care where that is—including to either one of you. Magdalene can be my only concern."

Keith says, "We didn't have anything to do with what happened to our sweet little girl, so look at us all you like."

"That's the thing," I say. "I'll be looking at you and your families and your friends. I'll be getting all up in your and their business, and that's uncomfortable and embarrassing—even for the most innocent of people."

"We don't care," Christopher says.

"Burn it all down for all we care," Keith says. "Just find out what happened to our little girl."

I nod. "And you should know . . . there are no happy endings in a case like this. No matter what."

"We know that," Keith says. "We know the chances of her being alive are minuscule. We just need to know what happened. We're not expecting a miracle. We don't expect you to bring our little girl back home to us and for life to return to normal."

"The horrific truth is," I say, "and I hate to be the one to have to even say it—even if she is still alive, there's no imagining what she has been through for the past year."

"We know," Keith says.

"I'd rather you found out that she is dead than that she has been abused and traumatized all this time," Christopher says.

"And finally," I say, "even if I can find out what I think might have happened to her—and that's a very, very big *if*—there's every chance that I won't be able to prove it. Not to the extent that a DA would file charges and prosecute."

"We realize that," Keith says.

"I won't attempt to punish whoever I think might be the perpetrator—no matter what he or she may have done—and I won't find and identify him or her for you or someone else to do that either."

"We're not violent people," Christopher says. "We're not looking to take the law into our own hands."

Keith nods, though I'm not as convinced he feels the same way. "We just want to know," he says. "We have to know what happened. We can't live with not knowing what happened to her."

I nod and agree to look into Magdalene's case, all the while thinking, *You may not be able to live with knowing what happened to her either.*

DAY 14

Day 14

The cops are making a big deal about a missing key card.

Because of how seriously we take security (wow, that's a joke now, isn't it?) we have all the key cards numbered and inventoried.

Two days before our solstice party one went missing.

We didn't misplace it or lose it. It was taken. Stolen.

One moment it was on the check-in desk—not on top of the counter but down underneath where we keep everything—and the next it was gone.

It takes a key card to get into our house. If someone doesn't have one, they have to be buzzed in. So the cops are saying this is how the abductor got in. And nobody wants that to be the case more than me. I mean, if someone was able to break in, that means we didn't do it. But here's the thing—Magdalene was taken on the night of 12/22, or I guess more accurately the early morning hours of 12/23. But the key card was stolen on 12/20. And as an added safety feature of the added security we offer (again, something that is ironic and cruel now), we reprogram our doors every day. Every single day without fail. It's automatic. We don't even have to do it. The guests have to come to the front desk every day and have their key card reprogrammed or they won't be able to get into the building, let alone their own room. So a key card stolen on 12/20 would be of no use on 12/22. And here's the other thing (and I keep telling them this)—it wasn't programmed at all. It hadn't been yet. So it wouldn't even have been any good on 12/20.

DAY 15

Day 15

It's obvious the police suspect us.

I guess I finally convinced them the stolen key card was useless and not how an intruder could've gotten in.

They think it has to be me or Keith or one of our friends staying here that night.

And I get it. Because of our security system. Because there is no sign of a break-in. Because the house was locked up tight when we woke up to find her gone ... It has to be an inside job, right?

But it can't be one of us. Can it?

None of us would harm a hair on her precious little head. Right?

There are no other suspects but us. But does that mean it has to be us?

And if one of us—who?

I wouldn't even begin to know who to suspect.

None of us are vicious child killers—do I really think she's dead? —or abductors, are we? Of course not. We're talking about my family. No one in the world is closer to me than these people.

But what if it was an accident? What if something happened— something the person didn't intend—would he or she or they cover it up? No. None of our friends would put me and Keith through that. They would tell us. They would know we would be heartbroken— but we would know. They wouldn't put us through the torture and agony of not knowing. They'd see how much it hurts, how mad it's driving us.

There's a theory or rumor being circulated that we gave Magdalene sleeping medication so we could enjoy the party, and that we accidentally gave her too much and she died of an overdose and we're covering it up with the help of some or all of our friends. They even say the cops found children's sleeping medication in our medicine cabinet.

We didn't kill our daughter. And neither did our friends.

But if not any of us, who? Somebody took my little girl. Somebody has her or knows where she is. Somebody, but who? And how'd they do it?

5

"What was that about?" Anna asks.

I tell her.

We are in our room, whispering to each other as Taylor naps on the enormous bed.

Each room in the Florida House is named for and themed after a famous Floridian. So far I've seen the Zora Neale Hurston, Henry Morrison Flagler, Harriet Beecher Stowe, Thomas Alva Edison, and Marjorie Kinnan Rawlings.

We're in the Ernest Hemingway room—inspired by his time in Key West. It's a huge room filled with what I'm assuming are replicas and what "American Pickers" Mike and Frank would call *repops*, but each item looks and feels original, antique, real. There's what looks like Spanish seventeenth-century furniture, a French chandelier, an Italian marble fireplace, hand-painted tiles, a white Chenille bedspread covering two full-size beds that have been strapped together in a manner similar to what Hemingway did, and an ornate wooden headboard that appears to have come from a Siglo de Oro Spanish monastery, just the way Hemingway's had. The room is so classically tropical, so obviously from an earlier era, it feels like we could step outside the room and be in 1930s Havana.

I quickly and quietly tell her about what happened to Magdalene and what Keith and Christopher asked me to do.

"They want you to investigate the case?" she says, though I've already told her they did.

"Look into it, yeah," I say. "See if I can find anything that's been missed."

"What'd you tell them?"

"That my talks would require a lot of me and that we were on vacation . . ."

"*But*?" she says. "*And*? I know that's not all you said. What else did you tell them, John?"

I start to say something, but she continues.

"Did you tell them you'd investigate it?"

"I told them—"

"I really thought this was a yes or no kind of question."

I open my mouth but before any sound comes out, she is talking again.

"What's over there under your suit coat?" she asks, cutting her eyes momentarily in the direction of the desk and the chair behind it where my folded suit coat covers the case file scrapbook Christopher made me. "You tried to be slick, but I noticed. You brought it in like you were sneaking a bottle of booze."

I tell her what it is. "I wasn't sneaking it in. I just wanted to talk to you about the case and my possible role in reexamining it before I brought out the book."

"Then do," she says. "Talk to me."

"I'm committed to this vacation," I say. "I'm going to spend as much quality time with you and the girls as I possibly can. But would you mind if I read over the case while y'all are sleeping? Maybe work on it a little as long as it doesn't interfere with our vacation or my talks?"

"Doesn't sound unreasonable at all, does it?" she says. "But we both know that's not all it will be, and even when it doesn't seem like you're working on it, you will be. You'll be thinking about it and figuring on it and letting it distract you from . . . us."

"Okay," I say. "I'll see if they mind if I take the casebook home with me and . . ."

"Answer me this," she says. "Is the case the real reason we're here?"

I shake my head.

"The main reason?"

"No," I say. "For me it's the talks and the vacation we get to have because of them."

"But you knew about it," she says. "You planned to investigate it all along?"

"I knew about it and certainly hoped to look into it some while we were here. Nothing more."

"Did it factor into you accepting the invitation to speak?"

I nod. "It did."

She nods as if this has confirmed for her what she knew all along.

"But not as much as us being able to get away from everything for a while," I say. "Not as much as it affording us the opportunity to have this nice vacation with the girls."

She doesn't say anything else, just nods thoughtfully to herself, and becomes even more distant, opaque, implacable.

"What?" I ask.

She shakes her head and shrugs. "Nothing."

"Something," I say. "And it has been something for a while now. What is it? What's going on? What can I do? How can I help?"

"What do you mean?"

"For the past little while—since shortly after the trial—you've seemed withdrawn, distant, unhappy."

"I have?"

"Come on, Anna. You know you have."

She twists her lips and they form a little frown. "I . . . I guess I . . . I'm not sure I have been. I certainly don't *know* that I have."

"You're saying nothing's going on?" I say. "That you're just the same."

Taylor stirs and we both turn to glance at her.

"She'll be up soon," she says, "and I really need a nap so I'll feel like taking her to the beach and entertaining her this evening."

"You won't have to do it by yourself," I say. "I'll help."

"I'm gonna lie down," she says. "Can we talk about all this later?"

DAY 21

Day 21

Where is the national or international media coverage? Why aren't the major news outlets camping out in the street in front of our house?

I don't understand. I really don't.

Why doesn't CNN want to cover our case? Or even the tabloids? I don't care who. I just want more attention focused on my little girl's disappearance.

Is it that they just haven't heard about it? Do I need to try to let them know somehow?

I read an article a few years back that said that the only missing or murdered child cases to get all the national coverage are little white girls—usually with blond hair. That boys and minority girls are ignored for the most part in favor of little white blond-haired girls. It also said that poor kids of any gender, race, or hair color are usually not covered.

But Magdalene is a little white girl with blond hair from an upper-middle-class family. She's beautiful and sweet and photogenic. She's everything JonBenet was without the creepy pageant videos. Is that it? Do we need video footage of Magdalene all dolled up and dancing?

We don't have creepy video, but we have video. Tons of video and pictures and we would share it with the media if they'd just come cover our case.

Or is it that she's adopted? Have any adopted missing children made national or international news?

That may be it.

But it's more likely that it's because Keith and I are gay. Who cares if two faggots lose their child—they shouldn't have had her in the first place. What's wrong with the world that two fruits can adopt a little girl? No wonder she was taken from them. It's God's punishment.

6

"It happened at Christmas," Keith is saying. "Christmas has always been Christopher's favorite time of year. We used to really do it up big, you know? Decorations for days. Concerts. Parties. Get togethers. Even caroling and shit. I was never into it the way he was, but, like a lot of things, he made me love it more than I ever thought I could. He says the Christmas season is magic . . . and he had a point. And that Christmas seemed . . . especially . . . magical. Everything had finally come together for us. I mean thing after thing fell into place—after years of not working out and looking like it never would, suddenly we were having Christmas miracle after Christmas miracle. That's what Chris called them. And I have to admit . . . it was . . . something else."

When Anna fell asleep next to Taylor on the giant bed, I had dug the casebook Christopher made for me out from beneath my suit coat and began to read it, feeling both guilty and excited to do so.

But then I had the thought that the best time to read the casebook was at night when they were sleeping and I couldn't do anything else. So I decided to take a look around the house and the property to not only get a sense of everything but also in hopes of running into Keith and Christopher. Hearing what happened from them—at least the first time through—would be far better than merely reading the reports and articles.

I had found Keith replacing the wood screws of the handrail on the steps of the back porch with longer ones. He said he was trying to get a few things ticked off his to-do list while Christopher napped and asked if I minded him continuing to work while he answered my questions.

"Up until then," he is saying as he turns the large-handled screwdriver clockwise, "we weren't sure we could make a living doing this, but it finally looked as if we would. We had each other. We had Magdalene—the family we always wanted. We had the business of our dreams. And suddenly one by one, like Christmas miracle after Christmas miracle, our families—the family members who hadn't already—began to accept us. I think it mainly had to do with Magdalene. Her adoption had just been finalized and she was really and truly ours, and I don't think my dad and Chris's mom—the biggest holdouts—wanted to miss out on being a part of the life of the only grandchild they were ever going to get. Chris and I are both only children, so . . . And I'm not saying everyone was completely accepting or loving toward us, just that the overt hostility was mostly gone, which in and of itself was a kind of miracle."

He pauses, takes a breath, finishes tightening the long wood screw he is driving, the muscles in his forearm twisting under a gleaming sheen of sweat as he bears down on the final few turns. He then wipes his brow on both of his short sleeves and starts on the next screw.

Keith and Christopher's home and bed and breakfast is on the very back street of Sandcastle. In front of it are all the homes and business and community buildings that make up the small, private community. Behind it, stretching for thousands of acres, is a dense pine scrub flatland forest, reaching back to Highway 98 and beyond.

"After several years of not being invited to Christmas at our families' places, we were suddenly the guests of honor and Magdalene had piles of presents under both trees. And it wasn't just our families. Certain old friends who had shunned us suddenly started getting back in touch. A few of our neighbors began to act more, well, neighborly. Even the social worker, adoption agent, and the foster family that had Magdalene before we did seemed to warm to us some. It was a real tipping point for us, and it probably would've happened anyway, but the fact that it was around Christmas made it seem more . . ."

"Christmas miracle-y?" I offer.

He gives me a quick smile and then the sadness returns to his face. "Yeah," he says. "Exactly." He shakes his head and frowns. "I shoulda known somethin' was up. There were too many good things happening. I shoulda been expecting it, had my guard up waiting for it, but I'd been lulled into some sort of dream state by all the lights and yule tide bullshit. I let my guard down and . . . just like that she was gone."

"Can you take me through exactly how it happened?" I ask.

He nods.

"Every year we have a big winter solstice Christmas party at our place," he says. "It's like the founders of Sandcastle—the heart and soul of the place. The people you met at lunch today plus few others. We always do it on the twenty-second of December no matter when the solstice actually falls. This place is a ghost town by then. We do it here and give everyone a room. People party until they pass out and someone helps them up to their rooms. Everyone spends the night."

I recall a snippet from glancing at the casebook.

On December 22, 2017, in the hours between midnight and

approximately nine in the morning the next day, Magdalene Dacosta disappeared in the night, never to be seen again. She vanished from her bedroom in the residence in the back of the bed and breakfast her dads, Keith and Christopher Dacosta, operate together in the quaint seaside town of Sandcastle. The master-planned community of Sandcastle is located on scenic Highway 30A, North Florida's premiere vacation destination for wealthy families determined to avoid the more seedy sections of this region that many refer to as the Redneck Riviera.

"How long have you been having the party?" I ask.

"That was our seventh year," he says. "It will be our last if we don't get her back."

"How many people in total attend?"

"It's very small and exclusive," he says. "We really do limit it to our close friends who run this place. Maybe four more than who you met today."

"And you don't have any guests staying here during it?" I ask.

"Usually, yeah," he says. "We make a point not to. But last year we had one guest whose flight got canceled. We explained the situation to him. Told him it'd be a loud, long night, but he said he was just going to put in ear plugs and go to bed. He had an early flight the next morning. And that's what he did. We didn't see him at all during the party and by the time we got up the next morning, he was already gone."

"Is his name and information and info for everyone else who was at the party in the binder y'all gave me?"

He nods. "Yes. Everything. His name is Hal Raphael. The police looked at him hard—like all of us. But our security cameras show him leaving alone. The shuttle driver said he was by himself that morning and airport security footage showed him arriving alone and on time and boarding the plane by himself."

I think about that for a moment. "So he was the only person in the house that night you didn't know," I say.

"Everyone else was a close friend, or at least close in the community or coworker sense," he says. "We had known all of them for years before that night and have continued to be close to them since."

"Did anyone's behavior change in any noticeable way after that night?" I ask.

"Yeah, all of ours did," he said. "We lost our little girl. They lost her too. She was like the community's child. And then at one time or another we were all suspected of the most unimaginable things—from murdering her and trying to cover it up to selling her to an international pedophile ring. It changed us all —and forever."

I nod and give him a sympathetic expression. "I understand that, and I'm so very sorry," I say. "But I meant did anyone start acting out of character—stop doing things they did before, start doing anything that seemed bizarre based on who they had been before?"

"I'm telling you. We all did."

"Okay. Go back to that night if you will," I say. "Please keep taking me through it."

"Early in the evening we had our usual candlelight solstice service in the chapel," he says. "Then we came back over here for the party. While Chris finished a few last things for the party, I gave Magdalene a quick bath and put her in her new Toy Story pajamas. They were an early Christmas present I'm so glad we gave her. She was so adorable in them. So huggable. I took her in to see Chris in the kitchen where she got a special treat for being such a sweet girl—a virgin version of the solstice punch— and then we both hugged her like a thousand times and I put her to bed. She was so tired. She would've gone to sleep sooner, but we kept her up loving and doting on her. The moment I stopped talking to her and hugging her she fell fast asleep. And for a while I just stood there watching her, then Chris joined me, and we were like pinching ourselves we had gotten so lucky. She was . . . just perfect. The most amazing gift of our lives. I don't know what happened to her or who did it. I have no idea what her life has been like since she was taken from us or if she's had a life at all. But up until the moment she was abducted, she was a loved and adored and well-cared-for little girl."

From everything I've read and seen and heard already, I truly believe that was the case.

"We stood there with our arms around each other watching her longer than we should have," he says. "Until the moment the first guest arrived. So she was in her room asleep before anyone arrived. None of the guests even saw her that night. The party started. We had a baby monitor set up in the kitchen so we could listen for her and we checked on her in person throughout the night. She was always sleeping soundly. Eventually we crashed. I'm not sure what the last time we checked on her was. It was reported that it was around midnight but it had to be a lot later than that. When we got up the next morning and stumbled to her room . . . she was . . . gone. All our guests were still in the house and it was locked up tight. And later we checked our security camera footage—we have a camera at the front door and one at the back. No one came to the house or left it—including Magdalene—the entire night. We were suddenly sober and wide awake and began searching the house and then the yard and area around it. And eventually the entire town. We were panicked and distraught and devastated. The police came. Took over. But we didn't stop our search. We didn't stop anything we were doing and neither did our friends. Eventually there were scent dogs and a helicopter and what seemed like a million cops. Roadblocks were set up. An Amber Alert sent out. But . . . nothing we tried . . . did any . . . . Our little girl was really and truly gone and we weren't getting her back. And that was something I knew from the very beginning. I'd never say anything like that to Chris—haven't said it to anyone until this moment—but it's something I've known since I eased her bedroom door open that morning and saw she was gone."

DAY 30

Day 30

I wouldn't still be here if it weren't for the incredible love and support of my family and friends. That sounds like such a bullshit cliché thing to say, but it's the absolute truth.

Clarence and Sarah Samuelson bring us food from their restaurant every single day—and they stay long enough to make sure we eat some of it. Keith and I aren't cooking and wouldn't be—and we wouldn't even be eating if it weren't for Sarah and Clarence. They've known heartbreak and tragedy and they know how to help those dealing with it.

My fitness friend Rake Sabin comes by a few times a week and forces me to go for a walk or a bike ride with him. I go kicking and screaming all the way but always feel better when I get back.

My bookish friend Wren brings me the best books on grief and loss and even books on missing children and how to deal with law enforcement agencies.

Derinda, Keith's mom, who has always been super supportive, has kicked into overdrive. She's truly amazing—the kind of mother every gay son should be lucky enough to have. Our adoption agent Demi Gonzalez and Magdalene's foster parents Brent and Charis

Tremblay have organized a search team for Magdalene, and Derinda hasn't missed a single outing.

Vic Frankford, our friend who owns the grocery store in town, brings by bags of food and household items at least twice a week.

There are others too—friends and family who help us in big and small ways.

And there are the strangers. We have received kindnesses beyond what I am able to describe from strangers. Cards, messages, emails, donations, care packages from people we will never even meet. It's staggering. And it gives me a hope for humanity that Keith says I am foolish to have.

7

As Anna, Taylor, and I are leaving the beach my phone vibrates.

I pull it out of my pocket and look at it, glance at Anna, then slip it back into my pocket without answering it.

"Who is it?" she asks.

"Someone I called while y'all were asleep," I said. "I'll call him back another time."

"*Who*?" she says again.

"One of the detectives in Magdalene's case," I say. "Roderick Brandt."

When Anna had woken up and I wasn't in the room, she had texted me asking where I had gone and what I was doing. When I got back to the room just moments later to find her still in bed and Taylor still asleep, she seemed put out with me. But we had moved past that and had a very nice time at the beach.

"Go ahead and take it," she says, and for a moment she sounds like her old self. "You'll be distracted thinking about it and wanting to call him back anyway. So you might as well take it."

I shake my head. "I won't. You guys ready for ice cream?"

Across the road in the town square, among the other restaurants, shops, and stores, is a sweet shop and ice cream parlor.

"*Ice cream,*" Taylor exclaims.

"I'll take her over to get ice cream," Anna says. "You take the call. Then we'll walk back together."

"You sure?"

She is already leading Taylor away and doesn't respond.

I withdraw my phone and answer it.

After a brief introduction, Brandt tells me he's more than happy to share information with me because he doesn't care who solves it—he just wants to get Magdalene back to Keith and Christopher.

He explains that he and Keith played football together in high school in Fort Walton and that he thinks the world of Keith and Christopher and believes what was done to them by law enforcement and the media after they had lost their daughter was unconscionable.

He tells me how much he'd love it if I could find her, if I could uncover something they overlooked, but he's very doubtful—because of just how baffling the case is.

"I'm tellin' you, that little girl just vanished off the face of the earth," he is saying. "Never seen or even heard of anything like it. It's like she never existed. I mean, I know she did. I know her parents and her foster parents and the state can produce evidence that she was alive at some point—pictures and records and whatnot, but . . . And I'll tell you another thing too. There's no evidence she was abducted either. Like I say, it's just like she vanished or was never there to begin with."

Late afternoon is slipping into evening. The sun sits low on the western horizon beyond the Gulf. Sunset at the beach has a quality unlike anywhere else I've seen. Light and color and sound are muted. There's a quiet calm—a serenity aided by the airy quality of the rhythmic rolling of the tide and the unabating breeze blowing off the Gulf.

"What do you mean by no evidence she was abducted?" I ask.

"I mean no evidence whatsoever," he says. "They woke up to find her gone. But their house wouldn't have been any different if they had just woken up to find her in her bed. None. We showed up to investigate. But we might as well have showed up to collect for the widows and orphans fund, for all the good we did. There were no signs of a break-in. There were no prints —well, there were hundreds of prints, it's a bed and breakfast —but there were no prints that meant anything to us. There were no signs of a struggle. All the windows and doors were locked. Security camera footage from the front and back doors showed that no one entered or exited the house during the night. Nothing out of order. Nothing out of place. Just a little girl missing. Gone in the night. And we have no idea how or why or by who. And now it's nearly a year later and we don't know any more than we did when we showed up that first morning. Tell you the truth . . . I thought we were going to find her somewhere inside the house. Like JonBenet. You know, something like that. We were walking through, searching—and it's a big place, so many rooms, so many closets, so many nooks and crannies—and I kept dreading turning the next corner, opening the next door. I was like, I don't want to find a dead little girl in Toy Story pj's two days before Christmas."

"I would think a bed and breakfast was sort of open," I say. "People coming and going all the time. Easy access for an abductor. On top of which they were having a party, so—"

"You can't enter the house without your room key," he says. "They're very security conscious. They sort of cater to single women coming to vacation here. And that only intensified after they got Magdalene. I thought you were staying there."

"I am."

"You didn't notice how tight the security is? You have to call from that little box out front the first time you arrive so they can let you in. And then from then on you have to use your room key to get back in the house. And they change the codes —you know, reprogram the keys every day so no one can use an old key."

"We actually arrived with Keith and Christopher from chapel so we just went in with them."

"Get them to show you the security measures and procedures," he says. "Or just try to get back in without your room key."

"I will," I say. "Thanks. So if no one broke in and—"

I see Anna and Taylor emerging from the ice cream parlor.

"Actually, can I call you back either later tonight or tomorrow?" I ask. "I've got to go get my little girl."

"Yeah, sure. ''Cause we haven't even gotten started good on this thing—including the aspects of the Florida House that might have contributed to the events. Call back when you can. I'm hard to get sometimes. Just leave me a message if I don't answer and I'll call you back soon as I can."

"Thanks," I say. "I really appreciate your help."

"You're the one helping me," he says. "I just hope you succeed where we failed. I've long since given up on a happy ending, but I'd like to see them get an ending at least. Some answers and some justice. They deserve that at least."

"At the very least," I say.

DAY 32

Day 32

I never thought it would go on this long. No matter what happened I thought we would at least know by now. Whether dead or alive, I thought we'd have her back by now.

Next to not having her, not knowing where she is or what happened to her is the worst. It's the losing of a child that breaks you —not just your heart, but your being—but it's the not knowing that makes you mad.

I know I'm going insane but I also know that there's nothing I can do about it. I can see it happening—almost as if it's happening to someone else—but I can't stop it.

With every day and hour and minute and second that slowly passes by, I'm faced with the cold, cruel certainty that we're never going to know what happened.

8

For all my concerns and suspicions about Anna, I know something is really wrong when she and Taylor step out of the ice cream parlor with a treat for each of them and nothing for me.

I had thought it odd when she hadn't asked if I wanted anything, but I figured she was just going to get my usual.

"Nothing for me?" I ask as I walk up to them.

"I didn't know how long you'd be on the phone," Anna says.

"Really?" I ask.

I give her a quizzical look, but she is already scanning the small town square.

The Sandcastle town square is a rectangular green with an amphitheater and recreational areas that include beach volleyball pits and a playground for kids, surrounded by the small shops, boutiques, and eateries that form the heart of the quaint seaside village. Like all the places along 30A, this planned community is unique and yet uniform, the architecture, color schemes, and overall aesthetic of every building—the businesses on the square no less than the residences beyond them—all conforming to and complimenting one another.

"I'll share with you, Daddy," Taylor says.

My eyes sting as her little hand shoots up, lifting her melting cone toward me.

"That's so sweet and generous of you," I say, "but I'm good. You eat it."

"Have some, Daddy," she says. "It's gooo-*oood*."

"He can go in and get his own," Anna says to her, then to me, "We're right here. Just go in and get what you want. We'll see you back at the house."

"You wouldn't even wait for me?" I ask. My voice is filled with surprise, but I can also hear the underlying hurt at its edges.

"Daa-*ddy*," Taylor said. "Have some of *mine*."

I squat down in front of Taylor and take a single lick from her cone. It's a disgusting mixture of bubblegum, mint chocolate chip, and peach with sprinkles on top. It's the best ice cream has ever tasted to me.

"Good, isn't it?" Taylor says.

"The best," I say. "Thank you so much for sharing."

"Have some more, Daddy."

"I'm good," I say. "You eat the rest. After you finish your ice cream, you want to go to the bookstore and pick out a book for tonight?"

"Yes, sir, please."

I turn to Anna. "I thought we could look around the town square while y'all finish your ice cream and then take her to the bookstore, but if you want to go back to the room and shower and rest, Taylor and I can meet you back there later."

"Are you going to the bookstore to get her a book or to interview someone?"

I frown at her and shake my head. "To get her a book and—"

"*And what?*" she says. "To—"

"I had thought we might get one too."

"Oh, well, I brought a few with me."

I nod. "So did I. Doesn't mean we can't add one . . . or two . . . or a few to our piles."

"We spend too much on books as it is," she says.

I shake my head emphatically. "No such thing."

"Our bank account begs to differ . . . and since you quit the prison . . . But you've already mentioned it to her now . . . so . . . I'm tired. I'm going back to the room. I'll see y'all there."

"We can walk you back to the room, get cleaned up, and then come back," I say.

Everything in the compact community of Sandcastle is within walking distance of everything else. The houses surround the seaside square on three sides, have no front yards and very little side and back yards, so are extremely close together.

She shakes her head. "That'd be silly when you're already here," she says. "Besides, I'll enjoy the walk back by myself and some time alone in the room."

"Then we'll look around at the town and give you some extra time."

"No need for that," she says. "Just do whatever y'all want to and have a good time. She'll need the ice cream cleaned off her before she goes into the bookstore."

I refrain from saying something sarcastic or snarky about the obvious nature of her comment and how well I take care of our girls in particular and books in general. Things are strained enough between us without me slinging some kerosene on the dumpster fire that is our relationship right now.

DAY 37

Day 37

I dream of Magdalene every night and I always wake up crying. Occasionally they are happy tears that roll out of the corners of my eyes to puddle in my ears, but mostly they are torturous tears that burn like acid from closed eyes that are seeing images no father should ever have to see.

I know now I will never get her back. Never get to hold her. Never get to kiss the damp hair of her head after her bath. Never get to cuddle with her in her soft footed pajamas.

She is dead. I know it. I can feel it in my bones.

I just wish I knew what happened and where her body is. I want to bring her home. Lay her to rest. Honor her short, sweet little life with a fitting memorial service and proper burial.

But I'll never even get to do that.

I'll never know what happened to her. Never know who took her from us and why. Never get her precious remains back.

I want to join her.

I want to die.

9

"You interviewing all the suspects?" Rake Sabin asks.

"What makes you say that?"

"Keith told me he and Christopher were going to ask you to help find Magdalene."

"Are you a suspect?"

"We all are," he says. "Every one of us who was in that house that night. And I guess one of us did it, but I have a very, very hard time believing that."

As Taylor and I were walking back to the Florida House from the bookstore, we passed by Wheel of Time, Rake Sabin's bicycle rental place—a large white tent on the town square with rolling racks of pastel painted bicycles.

He had come out to tell us that a bicycle rental for all three of us came with our stay this week and didn't we want to go ahead and get two now.

As we looked at and talked about the bicycles, I had asked him a few questions about the night of Magdalene's disappearance, which is what led him to ask if I am interviewing all the suspects.

"I only have a few moments," I say, glancing at Taylor. "Can we just start with what you remember about that night?"

Beyond the bike rack, Taylor is perched on a wooden bench looking through the book I just got her—a beautiful blue preschool picture book titled *Ten Magic Butterflies*.

"The thing is," he says, "I'm a health-conscious guy. I stay in shape. I bike. I work out. I take Taekwondo."

It is obvious that what he is saying is true. He's dressed in biker shorts, a tank top, and flip-flops, and his trim, muscular body is on full display. I'm not sure how old Sabin is, but it's as if his head is older than his body. His head, with its lined face, dark-circled eyes, and thinning hair, looks to be pushing fifty, while his trim, athletic body looks to be a youthful thirty-something.

"I'm not sayin' I'm like this big badass or something, but I'm no cupcake either," he is saying. "And here's what kills me. The one time I get to use it to protect that sweet little baby angel, my sorry ass is passed out. I don't drink. Except for one night a year, and even then I don't drink much. Certainly not as much as everyone else. But it's like this thing. Once a year at our winter solstice party I join in and drink with everybody else. And I guess since I don't drink any other time, it doesn't take much to get me buzzed or whatever. So while some sick motherfuckin' monster is stealing that innocent child out of her bed, I'm passed out on the couch drooling on Henrique who is drooling right back on me. That's what I remember most. And I feel as guilty as if I had left the front door open and driven the getaway car for him."

As he talks, I keep a close eye on Taylor, who is enjoying her new book immensely and even quietly saying words to herself that sound like reading.

"I'm very sorry," I say. "I can imagine how you feel. I've felt similar guilty feelings before. But maybe we can finally figure out what really happened, who has her, and get her back. I think that would go a long way to assuage your guilt."

"If we could get her back to her parents and if she was okay, I wouldn't care how I felt," he says. "But the chances of that are . . ."

Not good, I think but don't say.

I remain silent an extra beat, waiting to see what he'll say if I'm not guiding him with questions.

"We used to look forward to that party all year long," he says. "Now . . . it's not just that we could never have a party like that again . . . I'm actually dreading the approach of the holiday season. Can feel myself getting physically sick. Been thinkin' I might try to get away this year. This place is a ghost town in late December, so I could just leave. Drive to my folks place in Norfolk or my sister's in Gainesville. Hell, I'd go to my ex's to get away from here. Anyway . . . that night wasn't all that different from all the others—and believe me I've thought about it. I've spent more time thinking about those few hours than any other time in my life. The thing is . . . I don't want anything I say to make you think any of my friends are guilty, because I know they're not."

"I won't make any assumptions," I say. "Won't jump to any conclusions based on anything you say."

"I think we were all more tired that year than any other," he says. "We work hard all season long and the season here is getting longer and longer. But we're also getting older, so maybe that had something to do with it, but it didn't seem like anyone was feeling it that night. I don't know how long it went after I was semi-comatose, but it wasn't nearly as long as in the past. We've had many years—most—where more than a couple of us stayed up all night. Never me, but plenty of others. And you know how they say holidays are stressful? That's never been the case here. We're at our least stressed-out during this time of year, but . . . there was some definite tension. Not everybody had it, but something was going on between Keith and Christopher and Clarence and Sarah. I just figured it was normal couple stuff. And I still think it was. I don't suspect any of them. Especially not Keith and Christopher. They worshipped that child. Christopher is usually such a good host, catering to everyone, but that night . . . he was one of the first to sit down and not get back up. Just sort of like *fuck it I'm done*. And Brooke, who I'd never seen act like this before, seemed like she was high as hell when she arrived. Just sort of out of it, but not in a good way. It's like she was on a high but wasn't happy about it. She wasn't mellow at all. Just sort of agitated. I don't know. It was weird. But again . . . nothing that happened that night has ever made me suspect any of them."

I nod and think about it and we are quiet for a moment. Just because he thinks Brooke was high doesn't mean she was, but even if she was, I'm not sure it's relevant.

"I'm not trying to give any offense," he says. "'Cause I appreciate anything anybody will do for . . . Magdalene, but . . . Do you know how many different people have looked at this case? How many cops and detective and forensic specialists? How many reporters and investigative journalists? Hell, how many true crime podcasts and online armchair detectives and citizen sleuths? Do you really think you're going to figure out something none of them have?"

I shake my head. "Probably not."

"And if not . . . is it worth getting Keith and Christopher's hopes up?"

DAY 43

Day 43

I know now we will never get her back. There's no part of me left that can even attempt to pretend to the other parts of me that I believe she's still alive or that we will ever see her again. I've never known despair like this before. Hopelessness. No one knows this and no one will until they read this journal, but I tried to kill myself this morning. Maybe "try" is too strong a word. Maybe it was more just that I very seriously contemplated it and looked for ways to do it. I actually held Keith's handgun to my head for a few minutes before I found that I was too big a coward to pull the trigger. I don't want to live. But I am unable to kill myself. I just wish I knew what happened to Magdalene. Even if I never get to see her again . . . even if I never get to hold her . . . even if she's not alive and hasn't been for a very long time, not knowing is driving me insane. I just want to know what happened to her and know who did it. I'm not even sure what I would do about it. As much as I would like to think I would kill them, it's hard to imagine if I can't kill myself feeling the way I do that I could kill anyone else. Not knowing is the coolest torture ever conceived by the universe. I just want to know. Please let me find out what happened to my little girl. Why? Why did this happen? Did

I do something to cause this? Did Keith? Is this our fault? Did we let someone into our lives and into our home that put our little girl at risk? We tried so hard to protect her, but ultimately we failed. Maybe all those people who said we shouldn't be able to adopt because we are gay were right after all, but for the wrong reasons.

10

"All I ever wanted was to be a parent," Christopher is saying. "And for so long I didn't think it was going to happen. I say *parent* because I really always thought I'd be like a mother and a father, not just a father. My own dad was . . . Let's just say he wasn't what someone like me needed. He was distant, aloof, harsh, punitive. To this day he still hasn't fully accepted that he has a gay son."

It's late. The house is quiet. As far as I can tell we're the only two people still awake.

"I knew I could be a better father than he was," he says. "A better all-around parent, and I wanted the chance to be. We struggled so long to adopt. Turned down time after time. It felt like we were one of those fertility couples unable to get pregnant no matter what we tried, then having a miscarriage once we did. I had all but given up hope when Magdalene came along—and I think Keith long since had. But from the moment I met her I knew she was mine, meant to be my child. It was obvious to everyone—except for her foster mom, who was part of one of those 'homosexuals are an abomination' religious groups, but eventually even she came around. Unlike so many couples attempting to adopt, Keith and I didn't have our hearts set on getting a baby. We didn't care what gender or race, and we were even open to adopting more than one child in order to keep siblings together, and yet . . . we got our dream baby. It was . . . I think it was a miracle."

His voice is soft and quiet, his mouth dry. It's late and he's sleepy, but it's more than that. He's bone-weary and broken.

The weight of his sadness and grief haven't aged him any. He's so slight and has such a youthful face that beneath the bangs of his blond-highlighted hair he appears to be far more boy than man.

"I'd never been happier in my life," he says. "I had a husband I loved and adored and who loved me. I had a baby—a *baby*—a precious little angel baby girl who was heaven itself. We had a family. We were a family. And we had a business we loved. Everything was . . . well, it was perfect. It didn't last long, but while it did, it was perfect. It was perfect and it was Christmas—my favorite time of year—and . . . then it was . . . she was . . . gone. First we had each other, then we had her, and then we had everything. And then we had nothing. That's what it feels like. I mean, I know we still have each other and we still have our business, but none of it seems right now. None of it can ever be . . . what it was. The cruelty involved in letting us have her only to snatch her away is unfathomable. Not many people know this—maybe only Keith—but since it happened I have no sense of taste or smell and I've gone colorblind. Nearly a year now without smelling or tasting a thing and without seeing colors. I feel like someone who can't quite completely come out of anesthesia and everything that touches me or that I bump up against gives only the slightest sense of pressure. No real feeling. No actual experience of being awake and alive—just this limp, deadened thing without sensation."

His eyes are moist and his voice is hoarse, but he hasn't broken down and no tears are falling.

"Before all this happened, I used to be a big true crime buff," he says. "Used to read all the books I could get my hands on. Used to watch the films and TV shows, listen to the podcasts. Since it happened I can't . . ." He shakes his head and makes an expression like he might be about to vomit. "I haven't listened to even part of any show. I have no appetite for it. And all I can think about are the poor families—the husbands and wives, friends and siblings, moms and dads of the missing and murdered . . . And I think . . . I was never sensitive enough to their plight, never felt as horrified for them as I should, never grieved or experience grief for them to the level I should have. It was on some of those true crime podcasts and in some of those books that I first heard about you. It's how I recognized Merrick McKnight's name when I saw his first byline on an article relating to . . . to what happened to Magdalene."

He pauses and I wait, the desultory sounds of the large, old, wooden house creaking and the low hum of the central air-conditioning system momentarily moving from the background.

"I feel like I've been such a fool," he is saying. "You know how they say that insanity is doing the same thing over and over and expecting a different result?"

I nod.

"We've been trying to find Magdalene the same way, by doing the same things, for almost a year. It hasn't worked—*at all*. And yet we keep trying it. Keep doing things the same way."

He pauses but I don't say anything, just continue to wait while actively listening.

"Asking for your help is doing something different," he says. "New and different eyes on everything, a different approach to investigating the case."

"Probably similar to what's been done in a lot of ways," I say. "But certainly some difference too."

"The thing is . . . this whole time I've take such pride in the fact that even when the entire world thought that Keith and I killed her, accidentally or otherwise, or sold her into sex slavery —that not a single one of our closest friends, the ones who were actually here that night, ever believed it. And I've thought how much trust and integrity it showed that we never suspected them."

"You've never believed any of them could've done it?" I ask.

He shrugs. "Not really. Not more than a passing doubt or suspicion. Same goes for Keith. They've all been so loyal to us, so supportive when the media turned the rest of the world against us . . . I guess I thought I owed them the same thing. And it's been easy enough. I haven't really ever believed them capable of something so . . . But now . . . I want you looking at all of us like one of us did it—because one of us has to have, right? No one else could have. There's no other explanation. Our house wasn't unlocked, didn't have a basement window access with a suitcase beneath it."

I assume he's referring to the Ramsey home and the JonBenet Ramsey murder case from 1996.

"She wasn't home alone and we didn't find an open window in her room," he continues.

I assume he's now referring to the circumstances around the disappearance of Madeleine McCann while on vacation with her family in Praia da Luz in May of 2007.

"I've wanted it to be some fanciful explanation of someone somehow breaking in and taking her while we slept, but there's just no evidence of that. We're always so careful with security. Far more so when we had—when we got Magdalene. No one broke in. There's no evidence of that whatsoever. It had to be one of us. I can't imagine who and I don't know why or what exactly happened, but . . . when you exclude the impossible, whatever remains, no matter how improbable, must be the truth. The truth is one of us, one of my closest friends in the world, took my little girl. You can't imagine how hard that is to even say. As is often the case for an openly gay couple who are rejected or shunned by their blood relatives, our closest friends became our family, *are* our family, and I'm saying one of them did it, did this unimaginable thing. God, I feel so guilty sayin' it, but fuck 'em. Fuck all of us. Finding Magdalene is all that matters."

DAY 48

Day 48

The strangest thing happened today.

I'm not sure I can even describe it and I certainly know I can't explain it.

We were out in the woods searching for Magdalene and I began to get a panic attack. Derinda must have seen that something was wrong. She came over to me—quietly, cautiously, not drawing attention to me, not stopping any of the others from searching.

As she was asking what was wrong, Brent and Charis joined us, but instead of asking what was wrong, they both put their hands on me and began to whisper prayers. Soon Derinda joined in and I began to feel more love and grace than I ever imagined possible. It was like I was absolutely and completely wrapped in love. I realize I can't know exactly how this feels, but it felt like I was a fully developed child just before being born but still in its mother's womb. And she was the most kind and loving mother, so pure and joyful. It was as if she was love itself and that the embryonic fluid I was in was liquid love.

Eventually I realized that the mother was God and I was the child and that I was loved beyond description, that I wasn't being judged, only loved.

Something inside me shifted and I was able to let go of some of the guilt and shame and grief I've been carrying. I'm still sad, still broken, but I no longer feel guilty, I no longer want to die.

It was the most amazing thing.

Suddenly, I felt like if Magdalene was buried in these woods, it wasn't a bad thing in and of itself. They are blessed woods. They are part of God. Full of grace and light. This ground is as holy as a church cemetery.

I would never tell anyone any of this—not even Keith—but it was the most incredible experience of my life, and I will never be the same again.

11

On Monday morning Taylor and I go for a bike ride around Sandcastle.

I don't have a talk today, and I plan to spend the entire day with Taylor and Anna—and only work on Magdalene's disappearance when they nap or after they go to bed tonight.

There's a possibility that Susan is going to let Johanna come tonight instead of later in the week, so our entire family will be together again. I can't wait—even if it means that everything related to my talk preparation and Magdalene's case will have to.

Taylor is a smart, creative, fun four-year-old, but she is never more delightful than in the mornings.

We talk and play and laugh, and have a wonderful time.

In addition to the small, narrow streets of Sandcastle being conducive to bike riding, there are several bike paths through the undeveloped acres of scrub pine forest surrounding the master-planned community.

For the most part I am fully present with Taylor, completely attentive and focused on her fun, but as we ride through the woods behind Sandcastle, I can't help but wonder if little Magdalene Dacosta's remains are buried somewhere out here.

Additionally, I can't help but think about Anna and what's going on with her, and how it's affecting us. It's always in the back of my mind like a low-grade fever in an otherwise mostly healthy body.

"Daddy, what's wrong with Mommy?" Taylor asks.

Evidently I'm not the only one who's concerned about it.

We have stopped at a bench in a small clearing beneath an oak tree along the bicycle path in the woods.

"What do you mean, sweetie?" I ask.

I want to hear what's on her mind, what she has observed, what she is thinking, and what is concerning her before I say anything.

She shrugs. "I don't know."

She's looking down, sipping on the blue popup straw of her water bottle, avoiding eye contact.

When she doesn't say anything else, I say, "What do you think is wrong with her?"

She shrugs again.

Suddenly, this fun, carefree, wild-at-heart child is sad and heavy.

"It's okay," I say. "I know you love Mommy more than anything. It's okay to say when you think something's wrong. What makes you think something's wrong?"

She shrugs again. "She's . . . actin' funny."

"What do you mean?"

She shrugs yet again. "I don't know."

"What do *you* think it is?" I ask. "It's okay to tell me anything you want to."

"Are y'all getting a divorce?"

I shake my head. "No, sweetie, we're not going to get a divorce. You don't have to worry about that. Everything is okay.

Mommy's just . . . She's not feeling real good right now, but she will be again. Very soon she'll be back to her old self."

"Is she mad at you?"

Now it's my turn to shrug. "She might be. I don't know. But it's okay if she is. You know how much you and Johanna love each other and what great sisters and friends y'all are, and how sometimes you still fuss or get upset with each other a little? All friends do that. And that's okay. It doesn't mean you love each other any less or that you're not friends or sisters anymore."

She seems reassured, her little head lifting, her eyes actually drifting over to look at me.

"I mean it," I say. "Your mom and I are good. Our family is good. You and Johanna are safe and so loved and everything is okay."

She nods.

"Do you want to ride back into town and get Mommy a treat and take it to her?"

"*Yes*," she says. "Let's go get Mommy a treat."

DAY 51

Day 51

I had no idea so many kids went missing each year.

It's staggering.

As many as 8,000,000.

The truth is we don't really know exactly how many kids go missing. Some countries don't even bother to keep records of such things.

It's possible the number could be higher—much higher.

It's also possible it could be lower, but even if it's a lot lower, it's still stunning.

It's an epidemic.

Some reports say as many as 800,000 kids go missing in the US alone. That's 2,000 a day. Every single day 2,000 children vanish.

Others contend that the number is closer to 460,000, but regardless of which number it is, it's surreal. Hard to even imagine.

I can't believe I have been so naively cocooned in my own little self-centered existence that I didn't know any of this. It actually took my child being one of the missing for me to even become aware of the reality.

Even without knowing any of this, Keith and I knew our most important job was to protect our little girl, which is why we had and still have such an elaborate security system in place. But not even that was enough. I still can't figure out how it was compromised. It seems impossible. What went wrong? Where did we fail? Who could've breached the barrier of all our precautions?

Of the kids that go missing each year, whatever the actual number is, about 92 percent are endangered runaways, 4 percent are family abductions, 3 percent are critically missing young adults, ages 18 to 20, less than 1 percent are non-family abductions, and around 1 percent are lost or injured.

The so-called stranger abductions account for a very small percentage overall, but it's still between 4,000 and 8,000 children—as many as 30 a day.

15 to 30 children a day taken by a stranger.

I have to believe that Magdalene has to be one of them because nobody we know would do this—not to her and not to us.

12

"I believe I have you to thank for encouraging Christopher to keep a journal," I say to Henrique Arango.

He looks up from the book he is reading, *Havana Black* by Leonardo Padura, and smiles and nods.

It's the first time I've seen him without a hat. His cancer-bald head has a pair of glasses pushed up on it that he wasn't using to read, and it, like the rest of his skin, has an unnatural chemically created sallowness that smells like he just got out of too much time in a tanning bed.

Taylor and I are in the town square searching for a gift for Anna when I see him on a bench on the green and walk over to him.

I can tell he's about to stand and I say, "Don't get up."

But as befits a distinguished gentleman of a certain generation there's no way he can remain seated with us standing.

He pushes himself up, stands before me, and extends his hand—none of which seems particularly easy or effortless for him to do.

"Trust me, my friend," he says, "this getting old is not for cowards."

I nod and smile at him as I shake his hand.

He is definitely in the winter of his life, but his physical difficulties seem to be the result of something far more sinister than just that—not that aging and dying aren't sinister enough. No one has said anything to me, but I can tell he's not well.

"This pretty little thing has decades and decades before she'll know anything of that, doesn't she?" he says, bending down to shake Taylor's hand.

"Hello, Mr. 'Rique," Taylor says.

"Sweet, mannerly, *and* pretty," he says.

"Sorry to interrupt you," I say.

He shakes his head. "No interruption at all. I'm delighted you two stopped by to say hi. It's usually far too hot for me to read out here, so I try to take advantage of it when it's not. And among the joys of doing so is seeing friends."

"I just saw you and was thinking about how helpful having Christopher's journal entries are to my look into what happened to Magdalene, and I had to thank you."

"I've always found writing to be particularly therapeutic," he says. "I'm glad he took my gentle suggestion and I hope it was beneficial to him."

I nod. "There's no question but that it was."

"He just gave it to you?" he asks.

"A copy of it was included in a casebook he made for me."

"Fascinating," he says. "My guess is you are the only person to have read what he has written."

As we're standing there, Sarah Samuelson opens the door of her restaurant, The Sand Witch, and yells over to us. "I've just pulled a bread pudding out of the oven," she says. "Could Taylor come taste test it for me? I have vanilla ice cream to go with it."

Taylor looks up at me. "*Ice cream!* Can I, Daddy?"

"You'd rather do that than stand there and listen to us talk?" I say.

She smiles.

"I'll watch you walk over there," I say. "And I'll come get you in just a few minutes, okay?"

She lets go of my hand and starts running toward The Sand Witch.

"Be sure to thank her," I say. I turn back toward Sarah and raise the level of my voice. "She's very excited. Thank you."

"Our pleasure," she says.

"It's good of you to let her go," Henrique says. "They had a grandchild get killed a few years back—their only one—and they take every opportunity to dote on little ones."

"Oh wow," I say. "I'm so sorry to hear that. What happened?"

"I'm not sure exactly. They never talk about it."

I nod and think about it.

"Of course, we all know trauma and tragedy in one form or another, don't we?" he says. "Not possible to get through life without it."

I wonder if he's referring to his illness or something else— perhaps something closer to what Keith and Christopher are going through or what Clarence and Sarah Samuelson have experienced.

"I'm sure you know what I mean," he says.

"All too well," I say.

"'Man, born of woman, is of few days and full of troubles,'" he says.

I nod and smile appreciatively. "Job certainly had his fair share, didn't he?"

"That he did."

"Since I've already interrupted your reading and Taylor is busy getting pudding," I say, "mind if I ask you a few questions about the night of the solstice party when Magdalene was taken?"

"Of course not," he said, "but do you mind if we sit?"

"Not at all," I say, and indicate for him to sit down.

After he is seated, I join him on the wooden bench. Before us is a view of the green and all the activities taking place on it —children playing, couples sitting and lying on blankets, young people playing beach volleyball and frisbee, readers reading, families strolling, dogs being walked—and beyond it, the beach and the Gulf.

"What would you like to know?" he asks.

"To begin with," I say, "does anything stand out to you about that night? Anything different, unusual, off—that you thought of then or later after reflection."

"Not really, no," he says. "It was a pretty normal night for us, for our solstice gathering at any rate. Everyone comes to it exhausted and with holiday fatigue but also excited to be together and ready to party. We're more like a family than friends. We know each other very well and for the most part really enjoy one another's company."

"No one acted out of character in any way that night?"

"In little ways that don't mean anything, sure, but not in a way that signals they're a child abductor. Besides, Keith and Christopher already had Magdalene, so they'd have no need of abducting her."

"What was unusual about how they acted?"

"Nothing really," he says. "And it certainly wasn't suspicious. They're usually the most attentive of hosts—to an extreme really. This time they weren't so much. They seemed to be even more tired and stressed than usual. That's probably all there was to it. The holidays will do that to you. Plus they were new parents and probably weren't sleeping as much and still adjusting to their new situation."

"Nothing more to it than that?"

"You know how even when a couple acts or tries to act normal and even though outwardly everything seems fine you can still feel the tension and disconnect between them? Something was going on between them that night. I'm sure it was nothing big, but it was there. And it wasn't just them. Everyone was more exhausted and more stressed. No one was in a great place. It was clear Clarence and Sarah were having a tiff too. All couples do from time to time, don't they?"

"We certainly do," I say, and it comes out more enthusiastically than I intend it to.

"Both couples disappeared for brief spells during the night," he says.

"Not brief enough not to notice," I say.

"True."

"At the same or different times?" I ask.

"Different times. And Keith and Christopher did it a few times. The time they were gone the longest, they said they were going to look in on Magdalene, but when I stepped into the residence to tell them we were ready to open presents, they weren't there. But here's the thing . . . Magdalene was in her bed safe and sound. I could hear her soft little snore. And when I got back to the front parlor of the B&B, they were in there with everyone else. And they never left again until the next morning, so . . . I know they had nothing to do with it."

"How do you know they didn't leave the parlor again?" I ask. "Did you stay in there all night?"

He nods.

"Awake?"

"Mostly," he says. "I was in one of the high-back chairs. Just couldn't muster the energy and strength to get up and climb the stairs to my room. I'm sure I dozed some, but they were out—slept like bears hibernating all night. Everyone did."

"Did everyone stay downstairs all night?" I ask. "Did anyone go up to their room?"

"I think most everyone did stay down—between the parlor and the dining room. Some slept with their heads on their hands on the dining table. Others just sprawled out on the floor. But most everyone was in a chair or on a couch in the parlor."

"Is that how y'all normally do it?"

"In years past several of us would stay up all night and go up to our rooms as the sun was coming up. This year there was more catnapping and dozing. I'm tellin' you everyone was utterly spent. Oh, I think Brooke went up to her room and maybe Rake at some point. I can't be certain. But I'll tell you what I am certain of. I'm certain that none of us had anything to do with whatever it was that happened to that sweet child. I'm old and sick and don't have a ton of time left, but I'd bet my remaining days that none of us had anything to do with it. Like I said, I'm their alibi."

"Do you recall about what time it as when you went to Magdalene's room?"

"A little after twelve I believe. Why?"

"Sounds like you may be the last person to see Magdalene alive and well in her bed."

DAY 55

Day 55

It feels like the whole world has turned on us.

The investigators have indicated and the media has speculated that the person who took Magdalene had to be in the house that night.

They say there's no other explanation. There are no signs of an intruder, no evidence that anyone but us entered the house that night.

That means two of the suspects are me and Keith, of course, and we're the prime suspects at this point. The other suspects are among our very closest friends on the planet: Wren Melody, Brooke Wakefield, Clarence and Sarah Samuelson, Vic Frankford, Rake Sabin, Henrique Arango, Scott Haskew, and Jodi North. And, of course, the only stranger in the house that night, our B&B guest Hal Raphael.

Did one of these people, our chosen family, take our little Magdalene? It's just unthinkable.

It's much more likely to be Raphael, but our own security cameras exonerate him. As do the cameras at the airport and the Uber driver.

Could it be one of the others? The thing is, there's no more evidence that one of them did it than Raphael did. There is no evidence that anyone did it. That's the problem. Yet it was done. Our little girl is gone and somebody did it. Who? How?

The world, or at least the media covering the case, seems to think that Keith and I did it. They think we accidentally killed her, that we're covering it up, and that, if our friends are involved at all, it's in helping us cover it up.

13

I find Taylor sitting at a table with Clarence and Sarah Samuelson eating ice cream with sprinkles and whipped cream and chocolate syrup, the mostly untouched bowl of bread pudding pushed to the side.

"She's not such a big fan of bread pudding," Clarence says.

"Ice cream is another matter," Sarah says.

They are a middle-aged couple who have a relaxed manner befitting the beach. Dressed casually, they seem settled and assured and non-needy in that way that only aging and belonging and money seem to bring. They definitely have that ineffable quality that the wealthy have that indicates their lives really are as different from the rest of ours as they seem.

She is thin with long hair for a woman her age. Her hair, which is down, is thick and course and a light brown that looks too natural to have come out of a bottle. She is wearing khaki shorts, a white button-down with the sleeves rolled up, and leather sandals that reveal tanned, well-cared-for feet. Tortoise-shell reading glasses dangle from a dark cord around her neck.

He is dark complected with black hair and eyes, and looks to be of South American descent. He's thickish but not soft.

Like her, he's wearing a white button-down with the sleeves rolled up. He also has reading glasses hanging around his neck, but his are bigger and black. He has on designer jeans and leather flip-flops.

The restaurant, which opens for lunch in about an hour, is empty except for us. The floors are clean and the tables prepped and ready for the lunch crowd, which as I understand it is usually pretty epic—even in the off-season.

"Hope you don't mind us indulging her like this," Sarah says. "We can't help ourselves."

"Not at all," I say, then to Taylor, "What do you say?"

"Oh, she's thanked us several times already," Clarence says.

"She's such a good girl," Sarah says. "So sweet and cute and mannerly."

"Thank you," Taylor and I say simultaneously.

We are all quiet a moment as Taylor continues to eat her ice cream.

"Mind if I ask you a few questions about the solstice party while she finishes her ice cream? Keith and Christopher have asked that I take another look at what happened."

They exchange a quick glance then Clarence says, "We really need to get ready to open. We still have a lot of prep work left to be done and now we're way behind."

"Could we do it another time?" Sarah asks.

"Of course," I say.

"Y'all must come to dinner as our guests," she says. "Not to talk about the . . ." She mouths the word *disappearance*. "That wouldn't make for good dinner conversation, would it? But maybe after dinner we could talk some."

"Or a different time entirely," Clarence suggested. "The two things don't have to be combined."

"That's true," she says.

They both stand and tell Taylor goodbye and hug her, then rush off to the kitchen.

One moment they had acted as if they had all the time in the world and the next they rushed away.

"Sit and join her," Sarah shouts to me from the kitchen. "We'll send something out for you in a few. Y'all take your time and enjoy."

WE FIND Anna still asleep in our room, and when we wake her up, she lashes out at us.

"I'm on vacation," she says. "Don't be so goddamn judgmental."

I had jokingly asked if she was going to sleep the day away.

Taylor recoils. She's never heard her mother use those words or respond in this manner.

"Come here, baby," Anna says to her. "I'm sorry. I shouldn't've said that. I'm sorry."

She holds Taylor, who is in tears and still clutching the gift we got Anna, and begins to shed tears of her own.

"I'm so sorry," she says. "I was having a bad dream when Daddy woke me up. I wish he would've just waited for me to wake up on my own."

So I'm to blame for her outburst.

"What's in your hand?" Anna asks Taylor. "Did you get a treat?"

"Daddy and I got a present for you."

"You did?" Anna says, her voice rising and more tears coming. "Well that makes me feel even more lousy for snapping. Please forgive me. I'm so ashamed of—"

"It's okay, Mommy," she says. "Open your present. You'll feel better."

Taylor crawls off Anna and holds out the present.

Anna pushes herself up and uses the pillows and headboard as a seat back.

"You're gonna love it, Mommy," Taylor says.

"I already do."

"And it'll make you feel better."

"You've already done that."

"And Daddy too?" Taylor asks. "It's from both of us."

Anna uses opening the gift to ignore her question about me. "Oh, I love it," she says, withdrawing the snow globe from the ornate gift bag.

Inside the snow globe is a miniature Sandcastle town square complete with a sign that reads Sandcastle, FL.

"Shake it, Mommy," Taylor says.

"Okay."

Anna shakes the globe and holds it up again. Instead of snow, it's sand that swirls around the liquid inside it.

"That's *cool*," Anna says, and seems to mean it. "I love it. Thank you."

Anna pulls Taylor in for a hug.

"It's from Daddy too," Taylor says. "Hug him too."

"Thank you so much for this," Anna says. "You go wash your hands and face and I'll thank daddy and hug him. Okay?"

When Taylor is far enough away not to hear, I say, "She's scared we're going to get a divorce."

"You're not?" she asks.

"I wasn't until right now," I say.

"Well . . ."

"Who are you and what have you done with my wife?" I ask.

"*Your* wife?" she says. "I'm not your property."

"No, you're not, and sane Anna would know I didn't mean it that way."

"So now I'm insane?"

"You are if you think I meant in any way that you're my property. I just wanted to let you know how the way you're acting is upsetting your daughter so you could—"

"Oh, so she's just *my* daughter?" she says.

"Again, not what I said or meant and you know it—or you should. The other you would."

"The *other* me?"

"Do you not think you've changed recently?" I asked. "Drastically?"

She shakes her head and lets out a harsh little laugh.

I say, "Can we please figure out a way to talk about this before I go get Johanna?"

"Figure out a way?" she says.

"Find something to occupy Taylor and talk where she can't hear us?"

"All clean," Taylor says as she walks back into the room holding her still damp hands up.

"Good girl," I say. "Great job."

"How would you like to go to the beach with Mommy?" Anna asks her.

"Yay," she says.

"Go get your suit on," Anna says. "It's draped over the side of the bathtub."

"Yes, ma'am. Are you coming, Daddy?"

"He's got to go pick up Johanna. It'll be just us girls."

DAY 61

Day 61

Oh my God. It's unbelievable. I just can't . . .

I did an online search for sexual predators in our area and they are literally all around us. And not just a few. More than I could've ever possibly imagined. How can there be so many? And so close to us. Would it be this way no matter where we lived, or is this just here? Why the hell weren't we notified? We're raising a small child. Someone should've told us that we were doing so surrounded by a nest of vipers. Surely one of them is responsible for taking Magdalene. I want to go and knock down every one of their doors and demand they let me search the place.

How can the cops not be doing that? How can they not be looking at these known predators? And if there are that many known predators, how many unknown are there?

Has the whole world just lost its fucking mind? What is wrong with people?

I'll tell you this. If the cops aren't looking at these vile fuckers it's because of one and only one reason. It's because they're wasting all their time looking at us. They'd rather believe that Keith and I killed our own little girl and are covering it up—with the help of our friends I might add—than that a known predator somehow figured out how to breach our security system and get in and out with her without being detected.

14

A nna had told Taylor I couldn't go to the beach with them because I had to pick up Johanna, but the truth was I didn't have to meet Susan to get Johanna until later—Anna just didn't want me going to the beach with them.

Alone and with some extra time on my hands, I sit at the small desk, pick up the casebook Christopher made me, and flip through it.

Christopher's journal entries are raw and heartbreaking. Comments from Roderick Brandt, the investigator in charge of the case, show his frustration at the lack of leads. The local news articles and feature stories reveal way too much speculation and conjecture on the part of the media—particularly by the unsourced tabloid-type coverage found online.

Most of the tabloid and citizen-sleuth social media conjecture involves conspiracy theories ranging from the implausible to the outlandish. The dominant one, which actually claims to have a source close to the investigation, involves various iterations of a scenario in which Keith and Christopher gave Magdalene too much sleeping medication so they could party with their friends—friends who helped them cover up the accidental overdose and have since kept their secret.

In the pouch in the back of the binder is a thumb drive with a Post-it note on it that indicates it's the security camera footage. I connect it to my laptop and open the only folder on it.

The video files are labeled by dates and include 12/20, 12/21, 12/22, 12/23, 12/24, 12/25.

Each file begins at 12:00 a.m. and ends at 11:59 p.m.

I click on 12/20—two days before the solstice party.

A split screen shows the feeds from both the front and back doors simultaneously, each with the timecode near the bottom of the image.

Each camera is pointed directly down at the door it is covering, so it only shows when someone enters or exits the residence—nothing else. No approach or retreat. Nothing in the house or the yards. Only the two doors.

As much as I don't want to, as much as I don't have the time to, I decide that I have to watch every frame of every day—something I do at a sped-up rate and only slow down when someone is actually entering or exiting the house.

The angle of the cameras and the quality of the footage is poor to begin with—something seeing the video sped up only makes worse—but I can mostly make out the black and white and gray figures coming and going.

At 6:06 a.m. Keith exits the back door. At 6:37 a.m. Hal Raphael exits the front door. At 7:16 a.m. Keith enters the back door. At 8:11 a.m. Christopher exits the front door. At 8:13 a.m. Christopher enters the front door carrying mail. At 9:32 a.m. a couple carting luggage exits the front door. At 9:44 a.m. a woman pulling a rolling suitcase behind her exits the front door. At 9:57 a.m. a young couple and two small children exit the front door with multiple bags. At 10:37 a.m. a female UPS delivery person enters the front door carrying four parcels. At

10:41 a.m. the UPS delivery person exits the front door carrying a large parcel. At 10:59 a.m. a male food delivery person enters the back door pushing a handcart with several cardboard boxes on it. At 11:04 a.m. a male FedEx delivery person enters the front door carrying three medium-sized packages. At 11:05 a.m. the FedEx delivery person exits the front door. At 11:09 a.m. the food delivery person exits the back door. At 12:37 p.m. Hal Raphael enters the front door. At 1:26 p.m. Sarah Samuelson enters the front door. At 1:29 p.m. Brooke Wakefield and Wren Melody enter the front door. At 1:33 p.m. Keith and Magdalene exit the front door.

It's the first time I've seen Magdalene in anything but a still photo, which have mostly been headshots, and I pause the image and look at her for a long moment, then run it back and watch it several times.

Even in the short seconds-long clip, her energy and personality come through, bursting off the screen so vividly the footage seems momentarily to be in color.

She and Keith seem completely comfortable with one another, and appear enthusiastic about whatever they're about to do.

I withdraw my phone from my pocket and call Keith.

I tell him the period of time I'm looking at and ask if he recalls what is going on.

"That's the day we celebrated Christmas with my mom because she wouldn't be here on the day," he says. "While Chris met with a few of our friends to discuss the solstice party plans, I took Magdalene to play at the park and to the bookstore to pick up Mom another gift—a book for her trip. We had so much fun at the park. We were the only ones there. God, I'm so glad we did that. I just wish we would've never come back home."

"Thanks," I say.

We say goodbye and I return to the video footage.

At 1:46 p.m. Hal Raphael exits the front door. At 2:23 p.m. Brooke Wakefield exits the front door. At 2:27 p.m. a woman carrying a backpack enters the front door. At 2:32 p.m. Wren Melody exits the front door. At 2:40 p.m. a man carrying a large cardboard box enters the front door. At 2:57 p.m. Keith and Magdalene enter the back door—her with a partially eaten ice cream cone, him carrying several paper Sandcastle shopping bags. At 3:03 p.m. Sarah Samuelson exits the back door.

I'm not surprised to see Keith and Magdalene use the back door—any more than I would be Christopher—but I wonder why Sarah left through the back door, especially since she entered through the front.

At 3:07 p.m. a man exits the front door. He appears to be the one who entered with the large cardboard box earlier but it's difficult to be certain. At 4:17 p.m. a delivery person (I can't be sure whether the person is male or female) passes a package to someone through the back door but doesn't go in.

At 5:21 p.m. a man exits the front door. At 5:28 p.m. a woman exits the front door. At 5:44 p.m. Hal Raphael enters the front door. At 6:01 p.m. Keith's mom Derinda Dacosta enters the front door carrying a precariously stacked pile of presents.

At 7:26 p.m. a woman enters the front door. At 7:36 p.m. a man enters the front door. At 8:07 p.m. Hal Raphael exits the front door. At 8:14 p.m. a figure in a hoodie who could be male or female attempts to enter the front door. After a few moments he or she turns and leaves, and there are no more comings or goings.

Realizing this is going to take a lot longer than I thought, I copy the files and paste them to my desktop and then into my Dropbox folder, which I can access anywhere from my phone —that way if I find myself with a free moment as I'm doing other things I can watch the footage. Otherwise it'll take too long to get through it all.

I'm not exactly sure what to do about it, but there are

several people entering and or exiting that I can't identify. I'm assuming most of them are guests, but it's difficult to tell when they don't have luggage. And even when it comes to those I believe I am identifying, I can't be absolutely certain, given the quality of the footage, that I'm identifying them correctly—especially the ones I've only seen pictures of.

DAY 67

Day 67

My mom called today but instead of offering any compassion or comfort or sympathy she let me know that her preacher told her the reason Magdalene was taken was because my and Keith's relationship is an abomination to God.

So let me get this straight. God, who created me the way I am, is punishing me for loving Keith. God is love yet God punishes me for loving someone? Really???? Because I enjoy the company of and sex with a man instead of a woman, God has my innocent three-year-old daughter abducted?

It's truly amazing to me that one moment these people say that God is love and the next moment they're saying that he does things like this. And then they don't even see the contradiction. They don't even realize how inhumane they are and claim that God is. I don't know what we would do without Keith's mom. She has been so supportive of us. Always has been. From the very beginning. Hell, Magdalene's foster mom has been more supportive than my own mother. Of course our chosen family here has also been amazing, but that's about it. We really have no one else.

But by now we're used to it.

15

"I'm gonna be honest with you," Merrick is saying.

It's a little after nine on Monday night. We're in a booth in the back of the Donut Hole on 98 having coffee and pie. The restaurant/bakery is mostly empty and there is no one in the booths around us. I'm having key lime and he's having caramel. We're both having decaf.

"Wouldn't expect anything less," I say.

I've been here a while. This is where Susan was supposed to meet me with Johanna. When she didn't show, I called her and she told me she wasn't coming. Vague about why, she only said that she had composed a text to tell me she couldn't make it but had evidently failed to send it. It wasn't my week with Johanna, but I had been hoping that Susan would let her join us anyway because of all the fun she would have—and for a while it looked like she was going to, but maybe that was just to set up this classic passive-aggressive move tonight.

Extremely disappointed I wouldn't see Johanna tonight—I miss her so much when she's with her mother that it produces a physical ache inside me—I had called Merrick McKnight, my reporter friend who had recommended me to Keith and Christopher, to see if he had time to meet me. I then spent the next hour waiting for him to drive out here from Panama City. Fortunately, I could access the security camera footage from my phone so I didn't waste any time.

I was able to get to the end of the first day. At 9:18 p.m. Derinda Dacosta exits the front door carrying what looks like opened Christmas presents. At 12:37 p.m. Hal Raphael enters the front door.

"Calling you wasn't the first thing I suggested Keith and Christopher do," Merrick is saying.

"Oh yeah?"

"Yeah," he says. "First, I tried to solve the damn thing myself. I was like, this would make a great story for the paper, an even greater podcast, and one day a potentially bestselling book."

"Even a book," I say. "Wow. How many different ways did you spend the advance in your mind?"

"Too many not to be embarrassed about it," he says. "It's got everything a great true crime story needs—a seemingly impossible crime, little to no clues, plenty of suspects, sympathetic victims—Magdalene and her parents. I thought if I could solve it . . ."

"I know you don't mean it to," I say, "but it sounds so cynical and cold when you talk about it that way."

He nods and frowns. "I know, but I knew you would get that I was just talkin' about it from a story standpoint."

I nod.

He adds, "Hey, if I didn't care, I wouldn't've sent them to you. I sincerely hope you can find her—or at least find out what happened to her and who's responsible. I didn't get anywhere with it. Not really. And I honestly thought if anyone could it would be you."

"That's nice of you to say."

"I'm not being nice. I mean it. And it shows that I care. I'll help you in any way I can, but . . . I just don't have much to offer. I have no clue how it was done, let alone who did it. If you go just by the evidence it didn't even happen."

"Mind laying it out for me?"

"Not at all," he says. "Won't take long. The little adopted daughter of a gay couple goes missing on the night of their winter solstice party while only they, a few of their closest friends, and one guest of the B&B are in the house. The house, which is extremely interesting in and of itself—we'll come back to that later—has great security. Only guests with a room key that has been programmed that same day can enter the front door—and that only gives them access to the B&B part of the house, not the Dacosta's residence in the back. There are two security cameras—one covering the front door and one covering the back. Neither show anyone coming into or leaving the house after the party people arrived or before the B&B guest came out to catch his Uber early the next morning. And when he and the other party guests did come out none of them had Magdalene."

I nod and think about it.

"What can you tell me about the people at the party that night?" I ask.

He shrugs and frowns. "Probably nothing helpful. Have you met them?"

"Most, not all."

"To me the least likely to be behind it are Wren Melody and Henrique Arango," he says. "They're both pretty old and he has prostate cancer. But who knows . . . Maybe they're involved in stealing American kids and sending them back home—him to Cuba and her to England. I had the hardest time finding infor-mation on Vic Frankford, the guy who owns the little market. And I'm in the finding-information business. Something sketchy there. Brooke Wakefield, the hot young boutique owner, has continuous men and money troubles. Rake Sabin seems to be what he appears to be—a health nut and a confirmed bachelor. No red flags came up for Clarence and Sarah Samuelson. I'm not sure why they work the way they do. Running a restaurant is hard and they have enough money to retire and live large until they are 200, so . . ."

"Did they have a grandchild get killed a year or two ago?" I ask.

"They did lose a grandkid, but they led me to believe it was from disease. They lost a kid several years ago too. They still have three, but their oldest died while helping the dad with his boat—drowned in a storm and his body was never recovered. Definitely worth a closer look."

"Definitely."

"Jodi North, the Sandcastle rep theater director, is flighty and dramatic—or pretends to be. She's also broke. I think she's the only one of them who doesn't actually live in Sandcastle. Can't afford it. She commutes from . . . somewhere—Panama City or Fort Walton, I think."

"Haven't met her yet," I say. "Scott Haskew either."

"He's the director of the Sandcastle Foundation. They raise money from all the rich people living in and visiting Sandcastle and put on events and do charity work. I'm sure they're who brought you in to give the lecture series. I don't know this for sure, but I think he and Keith were dating when Keith met Christopher. I wasn't able to confirm that. Wasn't even able to confirm that Scott is gay. If he is, he's way, way in the closet."

"What about the only stranger in the house?" I say. "Hal Raphael."

"Every indication I got was that he was looked at very, very closely for it, but . . . there's just no evidence he had anything to do with it. He secures lease contracts for cell towers. Travels a lot. Seems like an average family guy. Single. Got a kid that doesn't live with him. If I'm remembering right he lives in Madison, Wisconsin. Keith and Christopher's own security cameras place him in the clear."

"If you go by that then they do the same for everyone else there that night too," I say. "And Magdalene never left the house."

"True," he says. "It's a real mystery. That's why I told them to call you."

"Do you have a theory?" I ask. "Or a sense of what most reporters who covered it believe?"

"I don't have any idea what really happened," he says, "but I can tell you most of the others think that Keith and Christopher did it and the others helped them cover it up. Like it was an accident or something and instead of coming clean they came up with this elaborate story for public sympathy."

"What did you mean about the house being interesting?" I ask.

"Well, it's interesting that it has such good security and this still happened," he says, "but I was talking about the other stuff."

"The themed rooms?" I ask.

"No. Have you heard of these escape room things?" he says.

I nod.

"The Florida House has one," he says. "And not just that but a series of secret passageways and some hidden rooms."

"Seriously?"

"100 percent," he says. "Keith's dad and uncles were builders and architects. He used to work construction. He may even have his contractor's license. I can't remember. Anyway, he designed the house to have all that stuff. It used to be a big selling feature of their B&B. They'd play games with the guests and . . . I'm not sure what all. I think they had this thing like if you escape from the escape room under the allotted time you get a free night's stay or something like that. I'm pretty sure they said no one ever beat it. Thing is . . . with all that hidden shit in the house you'd think it was used by the abductor, and maybe it was, but there's no evidence it had anything do with it. Still, you should get them to show it to you."

"I plan to," I say.

DAY 69

Day 69

I can't. I just can't come up with something to say today.

All I can do is cry.

My little girl is gone and she's not coming back and nothing else matters. Nothing else has meaning.

I hate this world. I hate myself and everyone else.

Fuck everybody.

16

As I'm driving back down the dark, mostly empty highway toward 30A and Sandcastle, I think about the case and wonder what I'm not seeing and why I'm not seeing it.

I'm disappointed that Johanna is not with me, but I'm still hopeful that Susan will let her come later in the week.

As I'm about to turn onto the road that connects 30A with Highway 98, my phone vibrates and I pull it out of my pocket.

It's Merrill.

Merrill Monroe, an African-American PI and community organizer, has been my closest friend since we were small children, and just seeing his name on my phone screen lifts my spirits.

"Man, it's good to hear from you," I say. "I miss you. There are like no black people over here. None. At all."

"It's expensive as hell to stay out there," he says. "And it's the beach. We can't afford it. We got no need to work on our tans. And we can't swim for shit."

"I also feel guilty for being away when everything is so bad back there."

It's only been a few weeks since Hurricane Michael decimated much of our town and county and region, and I find it difficult not being there to help in the recovery efforts.

"Be glad you away from this shit show for little while. They be plenty of misery and suffering for your ass when you get back."

"How's it going?" I ask.

"'Bout like you'd expect. We makin' progress. It's just slow as fuck."

Talking to Merrill makes me realize I've missed him more than I knew, and it hits me that it's because of how difficult things are with Anna right now. Not only am I not connected to her right now, but by being out here I feel disconnected from everyone.

"You okay?" he asks.

"Huh? Yeah. Sorry, I zoned out there for a minute."

"Your ass just solve a crime or something?"

I laugh. "I wish. Nothing like that."

"Well, I called to ask you an important question," he says. "Think you can zone back in for a minute?"

"Absolutely," I say.

"What you think about Christmas weddings?"

"I love Christmas and weddings," I say. "Putting them together is sort of like mixing peanut butter and chocolate for me."

"That's when Za and I plan to do the deed," he says.

Zaire Bell is a brilliant and beautiful doctor at Sacred Heart Hospital in Port St. Joe and Merrill's fiancé.

"Oh, Merrill, that's great news. Congratulations. I'm so happy for you."

"We were wondering if you'd be willing to do the ceremony," he says. "Tie the knot. Perform the service. Officiate. Whatever it's called."

"I'd be honored," I say. "Truly."

"Thanks," he says. "Wouldn't want anyone else to do it."

I wonder if he'd still feel that way if he knew the current state of my own marriage. I've already had one marriage fail—twice. If he knew that my second one might also, he might feel differently.

"You gonna tell me what's going on?" he says. "I can tell something's up."

I tell him some of it—enough for him to get an idea of what's happening without making Anna look any worse.

Even being careful, saying very little, and including very few details, I still feel like I'm betraying Anna, but my guilt is mitigated by how much Merrill loves and cares for and respects her. He's wise and insightful and supportive—and a very safe place for both of us.

"You the most caring and careful cat I know," he says. "You treat her like a queen and couldn't be any better to your girls. And you treat Taylor like she's your own. So even if there's room for minor improvements here and there—maybe especially when you deep down the rabbit hole of an investigation—there's no merit to what she's saying, so it's something else."

Hearing him say that does more for me than anything or anyone else could. Merrill is honest and not shy with his opinions—no matter what they are. And he's closer to me and Anna than anyone else. He's in a position to know.

A warm wave of relief and hope washes over me, and I am buoyed up in a way I haven't been in a very long time.

"How long we known Anna?" he asks. "Damn near our entire lives. In all that time, you ever known her to act anywhere close to this?"

"Not even close."

"Me either," he says. "So somethin's up. Has she seen someone—gotten a checkup or a . . . Sounds like that'd be the best place to start."

Talking to him and having him respond in this way does me

more good than anything has in weeks. I feel immediately better—just from having him hear me, from being able to share the burden of it with someone. And then to have him respond in care and concern for her.

"I can't get her to even acknowledge she has changed or that anything is wrong," I say. "She refuses to go the doctor."

"Then we go to Plan B," he says.

"Which is?"

"We get her and Dr. Za together. See if she can't subtly diagnose her over dinner or drinks to talk about our Christmas wedding."

"Thank you," I say. "You can't imagine how much just talking to you about it has helped me."

"Why your ass shoulda done it sooner and not make me have to drag this shit out of you."

DAY 72

Day 72

I still feel so guilty about that night.

I feel guilt AND anger.

My anger is directed at Keith. I'm mad as hell at him. Sometimes I can't even bring myself to be civil to him.

I don't want him touching me.

I can't stand the sight of him.

How much longer can we go on like this?

Every day I think, This is the day. He's going to leave me today. He will leave and I will be devastated and relieved.

What did I do to deserve any of this? Maybe Mama is right. Maybe it's just because I'm an abomination.

I still can't believe what Keith did, what he wanted to do. In one act he ruined everything. Broke my heart and took my little girl away from me.

Can I ever forgive him? Can I ever forgive myself? I thought I had, but it didn't last. Or it comes and goes—like everything else. Everything but the grief. It's the one constant of my existence.

17

L ater that night Keith and Christopher give me a tour of the Florida House.

"It's a very cool place," Christopher is saying. "Or it was until Magdalene was snatched from it."

We are standing just inside the front door. Before us is the large wooden staircase against the right wall, the hallway leading to the back of the house beside it, and to our left the parlor/reception area.

"I've always been into architecture and I love old houses," Keith is saying. "I'm especially fascinated by old mansions and castles with hidden rooms and secret passageways. And since we were building in a place called Sandcastle, I said why not incorporate some of those things in our B&B. So we did."

"We used to play it up," Christopher says. "Tell guests about it. Give them tours. Play games using the hidden rooms and secret passageways. Our Halloween haunted houses were the best. We even have an escape room. But when we lost Magdalene we lost all interest in it. So we don't even mention it to anyone anymore."

"If whoever took Magdalene used any of the rooms or passages I designed to take her . . ." Keith says. "I think I'll kill myself. I really do."

"Honey, we can't both do it," Christopher says. "Somebody has to stay around to be here when they find her, and I have dibs."

Keith smiles and pats Christopher on the back. "Let's both hang around and find her together. We ready for the tour?"

I nod.

Keith reaches over and pulls on what looks like a cord and tassel that go with the curtain and a moment later the steps of the staircase rise up, revealing another set of steps beneath them that lead down into an elaborately decorated room.

"Shall we?" Christopher says, and leads the way down into the hidden room.

I follow and Keith brings up the rear.

Down a short flight of stairs and we're in what looks like an old, formal study/library complete with huge wooden desks and tables, brass-studded leather furniture, and floor-to-ceiling shelves filled with leather-bound books.

Above the stone fireplace, the portrait of a medieval knight hangs in an elaborate and ornate wooden frame, and no matter where we go in the room his gaze seems to follow us.

The room is nice enough, but has a little of the fake feel of a TV set about it.

"This is our escape room," Christopher says.

"No one ever figured it out," Keith says. "We always had to come in and get them. There are four exits. Two behind bookshelves. One behind the fireplace. The one behind the fireplace is a set of stairs that leads up to the first, second, and third floors. The one behind the bookshelf on the left wall is a secret passageway that leads down the wall next to the hallway and opens through a secret panel in the downstairs restroom. The one behind the bookshelf on the wall in front of us next to the fireplace leads all the way back to our residence."

"I thought you said there were four exits," I say. "Does that count the way we came in under the stairs?"

"No, actually," Keith says. "I've always considered that the entrance since coming back through it doesn't constitute escaping the room. The other exit is just a panel behind the wall under the main staircase and it opens into the hallway. You have to climb up to it using something in the room—a chair is best—and you have to crawl through the panel, which is small and low where you come out."

"Who of the guests at the solstice party knows this is here?" I ask.

"All of them," Christopher says.

"But none of them knows where the exits are or how to access them," Keith says.

"That you know of," I say. "Just because none of them have ever escaped the room doesn't necessarily mean they don't know how."

"That's true," Christopher says.

"When you woke up and discovered that Magdalene was missing," I say, "you searched the entire house—including in here and all the secret passageways?"

They both nod and say they did.

"Did you show the investigators all of the hidden rooms and passages? Did they search them too? Did they have forensics process them?"

"Yes, yes, and I think so," Christopher says, then to Keith, "Do you know if forensics processed this room and the others?"

"I'm pretty sure they did."

"How familiar with the secret rooms and passages was Magdalene?" I ask.

"Very," Christopher says. "She loved them. We used to have the most epic games of hide and seek. She—"

He breaks down and begins to cry.

"Sorry," I say as Keith steps over to comfort him, wiping tears of his own.

"Don't be," Christopher says. "It just brought back such happy memories for a moment. I can see her running down that narrow passageway, her little arms pumping so fast, her little rear end waddling. And her sweet little voice. I can hear her shrieks and squeals and laughter. We had so much fun together."

"Yes, we did," Keith says. "We gave her the happiest life possible for the brief, perfect time we had her."

"God, I miss her so much," Christopher says.

"I know," Keith says. "Me too."

"We had her for such a short time, but it seems like she was a part of us for her entire life—maybe even our entire lives."

"It really does."

"I'm gonna step back upstairs," I say. "Give y'all some time alone. We can finish the tour of the house when y'all are ready or another time if that would be better."

"No," Christopher says. "We're good. Let's continue. This is how we do everything these days. Through tears and momentary breakdowns."

"You sure?" I ask.

"Positive."

They show me each of the exits, then we take the one behind the fireplace with stairs leading to all three levels.

The stairs are narrow and claustrophobic. Like the escape room we were just in, all of the hidden elements of the house are smaller and shorter and narrower than their visible counterparts.

We exit into an empty guest room on the third floor through a fireplace. It's the Marjorie Kinnan Rawlings room—the one that Hal Raphael had stayed in the night of the solstice party.

"Did Raphael know about this?" I asked.

They shake their heads and say he didn't.

"Did he go into the escape room or take a tour of the hidden part of the house?"

Again they shake their heads and indicate he didn't.

"Did he even hear about them?"

"Not from us," Keith says.

"He was here for business and really only slept here. I'm not sure he even interacted with any other guests, " Christopher adds.

"We really wanted it to be him," Keith says. "That would mean it wasn't one of us. But the security footage shows him leaving alone."

"The security footage also shows that Magdalene never left the house."

"That's true," Keith says. "But the cops looked at him hard for it."

"Then we have to look even harder," I say.

"*Ooooh*, I like the sound of that," Christopher says. "And I didn't mean that as gay as it sounded."

"Too bad," Keith says.

"We find her," Christopher says to Keith, "we'll make up for lost time."

"No we won't," Keith says. "We'll never let her leave our side again."

"True," he says. "Well, let's get back to showing John everything so we can get her back as soon as possible."

"Out here," Keith says, and leads us out of the room and onto the third-floor landing.

The hardwood-floor landing is roughly fifteen by fifteen. Five room doors, the staircase, and a small wall with a narrow table and a vase of flowers on it that stands beneath a huge gold-framed mirror.

The second-floor landing where my room is looks nearly identical.

"All three levels have this," Keith says. "A small hidden room with a passage that leads to our residence in the back."

He pulls the vase forward on the table and pushes on the wall next to the mirror and it opens into a small room with a narrow passageway that leads to the back of the house.

"It's nice when we're cleaning or working on the rooms not to have to go all the way to the front of the house and then up the main staircase," Christopher says. "Having these saves us a ton of time."

I nod and think about all the implications. "Do your friends from the party know about these?"

They nod.

"Somewhat. I'm not sure how much," Christopher says.

"No one knows them very well," Keith says. "Only three people do—me, Chris, and my mom, who helps us clean them and the rest of the house. But not only would she never take Magdalene from us—not under any circumstance—she wasn't even in the state. She went to my sister's in Washington for Christmas."

"But you don't think Hal Raphael knew about them?"

"Don't think so," Keith says.

"If he did, it didn't come from us," Christopher says.

Keith asks, "Do you want to take this passageway to the residence part of the house?"

I nod and we do.

The dim, narrow passageway takes us to the back part of the building, down a spiral staircase that reminds me of being in a Florida lighthouse, and through a door next to Magdalene's room.

"There's no evidence that Magdalene's abductor used this hidden passageway as far as we know," Christopher says. "But if they did . . . couldn't be much more convenient for them, could it?"

I frown and nod.

"I don't want to think about that," Keith says.

"Even if they did," Christopher says, "you're not to blame."

"I'm the reason they're even in the house."

"But, baby, that's like saying the architect or contractor is to blame because they put doors in houses and criminals entered through the doors."

"Well, not exactly," he says, "but that's sweet of you to say."

We are all quiet a moment, our eyes drifting back over toward the closed door of Magdalene's room.

"You've seen pretty much everything back here except for our bedroom and Magdalene's," Keith says. "Magdalene's is right here. Do you want to look at it first?"

I nod. "If you don't mind."

He slowly opens the door, and we carefully and gingerly enter Magdalene's room like we're trying not to disturb the dust.

Just a few steps inside, I stop and look around.

It is just as it was on the night she was abducted, except for anything the investigators and forensics team did and the addition of Magdalene's Christmas presents piled on the floor next to the wall near the door.

Her small big-girl bed is still unmade, the pink princess comforter turned back to reveal white sheets with little pink flowers on them.

Instead of a closet she has an antique armoire, the doors of which are open enough to reveal an extensive and extravagant wardrobe, by turns cutesy and casual, fashionable and formal.

Toys are scattered throughout the room—mostly in a semi-orderly fashion.

A tiny table with small chairs sits in the far corner. A huge teddy bear in one of the chairs looks lonely and about to topple onto the floor. The table is covered with paper and pens, markers and crayons, and some of Magdalene's work—one particularly poignant creation has three stick figures, a little girl standing between two men, their long noodle arms twisting around to hold each other's hands. Crayon scrawl reads "I love my Dads."

Several places throughout the room still have a dusting of black fingerprint powder on them—including the bedposts and doorjambs.

A few of the drawers of her dresser are open and have clothes spilling out.

"We always kept her room neat and clean," Christopher says. "And she was pretty good about it too. Especially for her age. The open drawers and that dirty-looking black powder are from the police. I need to clean it. Just haven't been able to. This is the longest I've been in here since it happened."

"There's no rush," Keith says. "We'll get to it when we're able."

The room reveals evidence of a loved and adored and cared-for and indulged little girl.

On the wall above the headboard of the bed is a large black-and-white poster of a youngish Dolly Parton. She has large hoop earrings and a ribbon in her big blond hair and she is looking off to the side pensively, her mouth barely open as if in the moment before she says something.

Keith says, "Chris is a closeted country music fan. Something he quickly passed on to Magdalene."

"Queen Dolly transcends country music," Christopher says, "and is a great role model for anyone—especially a little girl with two dads. Her energy and vibe, her talent, her work ethic, her positivity, her graciousness and generosity and self-depre-cation. I can't believe we're not going to get to see the woman Magdalene would have grown up to be."

On the bedside table is a Dolly Parton makeup set.

"The night before . . . before we lost her," Christopher says, "she had me paint her nails—fingers and toes—all in the same Hard Candy Apple Red Christmas. I knocked the bottle over and spilled some on the sleeve of her new Toy Story pajamas. She was so good about it. I promised I'd get her more of both—the nail polish and the pajamas. She didn't care. Only thing she cared about was not having to take those pj's off. She insisted on keeping them on, Hard Candy Apple Red Christmas stain and all."

"And I'm glad we let her," Keith says.

"*Let her*," Christopher says. "That's cute."

I glance over at the pile of unopened Christmas presents, which is huge. Next to them is a smaller pile of opened presents.

"That's not just from us," Keith says. "Those are the ones from my mom and her foster mom and our friends. We all went a little overboard."

"It was our first Christmas with her," Christopher says. "Everyone was so happy for us—even those who weren't at first. It was going to be . . ."

He breaks down again.

"Why are some opened?" I ask.

Keith says, "My mom went to my sister's in Washington for Christmas, so we had Christmas with her early. It was . . . I guess it had to be two days before the party because her flight was the day before the party. Magdalene got to open her presents from her grandma then."

"And one from us," Christopher says between sobs, "the Toy Story pajamas she was sleeping in the night she—" He turns and rushes out of the room.

Keith follows him.

I linger for a moment longer.

God, please help me find this sweet little girl alive and return her to her parents. Please.

"I'm so sorry we live in a world where you can be put up for adoption and be abducted," I say to Magdalene. "But I'm going to do everything I can to find you and . . ."

I'm not sure what else to say. I was going to say *bring to justice whoever took you*, but there is no justice for something like that, so I just let the unfinished sentence hang there in the air, suspended like Magdalene's unfinished life.

DAY 75

Day 75
I have nothing to say. Literally, nothing.
I committed to write in this journal every day, so here it is.
What I have to say today is NOTHING.

18

On Tuesday morning I give a brief lecture and participate in a talkback on the American criminal justice system and the need for reform, with an emphasis on the prison system.

Both the talk and the Q&A seem well received. The questions are thoughtful and the discussion good. The most surprising thing about any of it is Anna's decision not to attend. She informed me last night that she and Taylor would sleep in, then go to the beach, grab some lunch, and see me back at the room later in the day. But when I was getting ready this morning Taylor let her mama know she wanted to go with me.

So I get the pleasure of Taylor's company and Anna gets a day to herself.

Following the talkback I am introduced to several people—including Keith's mom Derinda Dacosta and Scott Haskew, executive director of the Sandcastle Foundation, the not-for-profit group that supports educational and charitable events in Sandcastle and Walton County. He's one of two people that I haven't met yet who were at the solstice party the night Magdalene was taken. The other, Jodi North, is also present and I am introduced to her too. An overly dramatic aging actress, North is the creative director of the Sandcastle Repertory Theater.

I also meet Magdalene's former foster parents Brent and Charis Tremblay, and the adoption agent who was so helpful to Christopher and Keith, Demi Gonzalez.

The crowd for my second talk is far larger than my first because every Tuesday for the past several months, Keith and Christopher's family, friends, and a group of so-called citizen sleuths descend on Sandcastle to join locals in a methodical search for Magdalene.

Many of the shopkeepers close early on Tuesday afternoons to also join the search. The well-organized and motivated group has created a grid that extends out from the Florida House and each week are combing through another quadrant, looking not only for Magdalene but also for clues to her disappearance.

"Do you two participate in the searches for Magdalene on Tuesdays?" I ask Scott Haskew and Jodi North, who happen to be standing near me as people mill about in the chapel after the talkback.

"I wish I could," Haskew says, "but . . . these days I'm largely a staff of one, and I can never seem to get caught up."

"Same here, darling," Jodi says. "Nobody seems to understand what it takes to operate such a fine regional repertory theater as ours."

As I talk to people about the lecture I've just given and look for opportunities to interview the suspects in Magdalene's disappearance, Derinda Dacosta sits next to Taylor on the front row, interacting animatedly and assisting her in the activities book she brought for entertainment.

"But you were there at the party the night Magdalene was taken?" I say.

Haskew nods.

"Disappeared," Jodi North corrects. "The night the poor dear *disappeared*. We don't know for certain she was taken."

"What do you mean?" I ask.

"Only that as I understand it there's no evidence she was abducted," she says. "That's all. All we know for sure is that she's gone."

"Well, if she wasn't taken, how did she disappear?"

"I'm sure I don't know," she says. "But I do know there are more things in heaven and on earth than are dreamt of in your philosophy."

"Meaning something inexplicable?" I ask. "Spiritual perhaps?"

She shrugs, and she does it like she does everything—dramatically. "Perhaps. Sandcastle is built on top of an ancient temple mound. There's much that goes on here that we can't explain. But I wasn't referring to that as much as the possibility that she wasn't *taken* so much as *hidden*."

Haskew gives her a slight shake of the head and roll of his eyes.

"Hidden?" I ask.

"That house is so big and has so many rooms—many of them hidden. So many passageways—some of them secret. Isn't it at least possible that the poor dear never left the house?"

Haskew says, "Sandcastle is not built on an ancient temple mound. That's been proven to be much farther inland. And that house has been searched more than a Muslim air traveler since 9-11. Y'all excuse me, please. I need to have a word with the Samuelsons about our foundation luncheon."

As he moves away, Wren Melody, the British bookstore owner, and Brooke Wakefield, the thin, platinum-blond boutique owner, drift over.

"Oh, Jodi, did you get my message?" Wren says. "I left it on your mobile when I didn't get you."

Jodi shakes her head.

"The book of Harold Pinter plays you ordered arrived today," Wren says. "I should've brought it with me this morning, but I came straight 'round here instead of popping into the bookstore first, didn't I?"

"Marvelous," Jodi says. "I'll stop by this afternoon and pick it up."

"I have to say," Wren says, "I'm absolutely delighted you're considering going with a Brit for your next production."

"Two, actually," Jodi says. "Shakespeare and Pinter. We're thinking *Much Ado about Nothing* and *The Birthday Party*."

"Oh, excellent," Wren says. "Well done, you. Cheers. Speaking of well done . . ." She turns toward me. "Another great talk, dear boy."

"Thank you."

Brooke Wakefield nods enthusiastically, her straight-haired, platinum-blond head bobbing up and down, her large earrings making tiny tinkling sounds as she does. "Really good," she says.

I start to thank her, but she steps forward into the small circle the four of us have formed, lowers her voice and says, "I'd prefer this to stay between us, but my brother's in prison, and I know firsthand how difficult, inhumane, and unjust it all can be."

She doesn't look like someone who has a brother in prison. Not that there's a look, but if there were, she wouldn't have it. From the tip of her platinum-blond hair to the tips of her manicured toes she appears to have been put together for a high-end fashion shoot.

I had been told she comes from money—that, in fact, her wealthy family had not only set her up in the boutique business here in Sandcastle but also supplements her income so she can continue to live in the manner they raised her to be accustomed to.

"No system is perfect, of course," Wren says, "but as good in theory as America's is, it's not nearly as good as most Americans think it is."

"I can guarantee that the Americans who think it's the best haven't had any dealings with it," Brooke says. "As a victim or someone accused of a crime."

"Or," Wren says, nodding toward me, "someone who has worked within it."

Jodi leans in and starts to say something but stops as Keith and his mom walk up.

"John, did you meet my mom, Derinda?" Keith asks.

"We met a few minutes ago, honey," Derinda says. "But you've met so many new people in the last few days it's got to be hard to remember. I'm Derinda Dacosta. Keith and Christopher's mom and Magdalene's grandmother. And your daughter is delightful."

Though you can still see the beauty she must have been, Derinda Dacosta now has the roundish, matronly look of a middle-aged woman with a pampered, sedentary lifestyle. Covering her overly ample bosom and the other round shapes beneath it are the middle-aged clothes of a schoolmarm who when she updates her wardrobe at all it's in favor of comfortable bargains instead of stylish elegance. None of which would stand out so extremely if she weren't standing next to Brooke.

"Of course I remember you," I say. "Good to see you again. And thank you," I add, glancing at Taylor who is being very patient but is clearly ready to go.

Keith motions over Brent and Charis Tremblay and Demi Gonzalez.

"Will you be able to join us in the search this afternoon?" Derinda asks me.

"I plan to," I say. "But I've promised my wife some extra family time and I have to pick up my other daughter this evening, so I'm not sure how long I can stay."

"Every little bit helps," she says. "Here's the two ladies who we have to thank for these weekly searches right here."

As Brent and Charis and Demi join our expanding circle, I notice that without saying anything Jodi has eased out of it.

"Don't forget Brent," Charis says. "He helped organize it too."

"*Helped, hell*," Demi says. "He *was* the organization. Wouldn't have any if it weren't for him."

Brent extended his hand and I shook it. "Just wanted to let you know I enjoyed your talk," he says. "I'm afraid I have a meeting in Mobile this afternoon so I'm about to have to leave."

"Thank you," I say. "I appreciate that."

He's a short, slight man with soft hands and a Caucasian fro.

"It was so good of y'all to start the weekly search," I say.

"We had to do something," Charis says. "Like everyone else, including poor Keith and Christopher, we felt so helpless."

Demi says, "We were thinking about what we might do to help—even in some small way—and Charis said how about a search."

"I didn't think a completely thorough search of the area had ever been done," Charis says. "And in every crime show I've ever seen they always do a careful and methodical search for . . . clues."

"The woods behind Keith and Christopher's house is so big," Derinda says. "And it had never been properly searched."

"So," Demi says, "we decided to do one ourselves. We studied how to do it and Brent helped us create a grid and a system for searching it."

"It's taking us a while to work our way through it," Charis says, "but we're getting there, and we didn't feel like we could ask our volunteers for more than one afternoon a week."

"Since we started," Demi says, "our number keeps growing. Friends and family. Citizen sleuths. And people who live here in Sandcastle. Several of the stores close early on Tuesdays so their owners and employees can help us."

"We may be wasting our time," Charis says, "but we don't know what else to do. And we're not just looking for Magdalene. We're searching for clues—anything that might tell us what happened to her that night, who took her, which direction they may have gone, anything at all that might help us find her. Plus if nothing else we're keeping attention focused on her disappearance."

DAY 93

Day 93

I know they mean well, but I really can't take Clarence and Sarah Samuelson telling me how much they can relate to what I'm going through because they lost a grandchild of their own. They don't know what I'm going through and even if they did, so what? How is that supposed to help me? I just don't know what I'm supposed to do with that. But they act like we have this bond now, like we're supposed to be so close.

They think we have so much in common because we both lost someone, but I waited my entire life to have a child. And it really does feel like my entire life, but even if you want to just say my entire adult life, I've wanted to be a dad or dad and a mom for a very very very very very very very long time. They can't possibly know what I'm going through. I would never say something like that to someone else.

I know they really do mean well, but sometimes it feels like they're just using me and my grief.

In some ways I feel like they must feel guilty—at least that's what they sound like—and I wonder if they had something to do with the loss of their grandchild.

19

W hen Taylor and I get back from the chapel talk, Anna is visibly frustrated. As she helps Taylor get her swimsuit on she expresses that frustration. Why were we so late. We must have gone somewhere afterward —no doubt to interview someone about Magdalene's disappearance. Why does everything always have to be on my schedule. I cost her valuable beach time because I'm selfish and inconsiderate.

As I listen, I wonder again what happened to my sweet, supportive wife. She really doesn't even seem like the same person.

Several times I start to challenge what she's saying, but each time decide that as bad as it is for Taylor to being hearing all this, it would be worse for her to witness an argument.

"You didn't have to wait for me, Mommy," Taylor says. "You could've gone without me. I wouldn't mind."

"I was happy to wait on you, sweet girl," Anna says.

Happy is not how I would describe the way in which she waited.

"You didn't do anything wrong," I say to Taylor.

"You didn't either, Daddy," she says.

"Okay," Anna says. "You're all ready. It's beach time. Let's go."

I give Taylor a hug. As I do, Anna quickly picks up her beach bag and cooler, and when I attempt to hug her uses them as shields to block me.

When they are gone, I change clothes and get ready to go join the search. As I do, I pray for Anna, for answers and healing, to get my wife back. I then pray that I will have the patience and the grace to be kind and loving no matter what she says or does—something I'm too often failing at these days.

Realizing I have a few extra moments before I need to leave, I sit at the small desk, open my laptop, and begin watching the security camera footage again.

I open the file named 12/21.

At 5:56 a.m. Keith exits the back door. At 6:47 a.m. Hal Raphael exits the front door. At 7:11 a.m. Keith enters the back door. At 10:15 a.m. Christopher exits the front door. At 10:18 a.m. Christopher enters the front door carrying mail.

At 10:57 a.m. a female UPS delivery person enters the front door carrying a tall stack of parcels. At 11:01 a.m. the UPS delivery person exits the front door carrying several small parcels. At 11:29 a.m. a male FedEx delivery person enters the front door carrying four medium-sized packages and three small ones. At 11:35 a.m. the FedEx delivery person exits the front door with two large packages. At 11:09 a.m. Scott Haskew and Henrique Arango enter the front door. At 12:33 p.m. Hal Raphael enters the front door. At 1:27 p.m. Hal Raphael exits the front door. At 1:33 p.m. Henrique Arango exits the front door.

At 2:27 p.m. a woman carrying a backpack exits the front door.

At 3:17 p.m. a young man exits the front door. At 4:21 p.m. Scott Haskew exits the front door. At 5:28 p.m. Hal Raphael enters the front door carrying two plastic shopping bags.

At 9:26 p.m. Hal Raphael exits the front door.

I open the file named 12/22.

At 6:16 a.m. Keith exits the back door. At 6:17 a.m. Hal Raphael enters the front door. At 7:17 a.m. Keith enters the back door. At 7:19 a.m. Hal Raphael exits the front door. At 10:17 a.m. Christopher exits the front door. At 10:21 a.m. Christopher enters the front door carrying mail that includes a newspaper and a few packages.

At 11:07 a.m. a female UPS delivery person enters the front door carrying several parcels. At 11:11 a.m. the UPS delivery person exits the front door carrying a few small and medium parcels. At 11:39 a.m. a male FedEx delivery person enters the front door carrying a single medium-sized package. At 11:43 a.m. the FedEx delivery person exits the front door with two large packages. At 12:09 a.m. Scott Haskew enters the front door. At 12:37 p.m. Hal Raphael enters the front door. At 1:17 p.m. Rake Sabin enters the front door. At 1:33 p.m. Charis Tremblay enters the front door carrying several Christmas gifts. At 1:43 p.m. Demi Gonzalez enters the front door carrying three small Christmas gifts. At 1:51 p.m. Sarah Samuelson and Brooke Wakefield enter the front door carrying large cardboard boxes of what looks to be decorations.

Glancing at the time at the top of the screen, I realize I'm running late. Closing the computer, I jump up, and rush out the door.

I ARRIVE at the staging area to find a loving and supportive group of dedicated volunteer searchers who rather than being overly earnest and somber are upbeat and jovial.

Clarence and Sarah Samuelson, the owners of The Sand Witch, have tables of food and drinks set up and are serving everyone in a manner reminiscent of the way the gracious and generous angels of mercy have been back home in the aftermath of Michael.

"Would you like a gourmet grilled cheese and a cup of tomato basil soup?" Sarah asks as I approach the table.

I remember that I haven't eaten anything today and realize how hungry I am.

"Sure," I say. "Thank you. This is incredibly generous of you."

"It's the least we can do," Clarence says.

"Where's that cute little girl of yours?" Sarah asks.

"She and her mom are headed down to the beach."

"We sure enjoyed our time with her yesterday," Clarence says. "What a bright, sweet, mannerly little girl."

"Thank you," I say. "She enjoyed y'all."

"She enjoyed our ice cream," Clarence says. "We know what's what."

"You feed the volunteers every time they search?" I ask.

"Feed them then help search," Sarah says.

"It's the least we can do," Clarence says. "The time we could've done more than the least we can do was that night."

He doesn't have to say any more than that for me or anyone else to know which night he's talking about.

"That poor little darling," Sarah says. "I can't believe that I . . . that I didn't . . . wake up. I'm usually such a light sleeper."

"We drank too much," Clarence says.

She nods slowly and frowns. "I suppose so."

"Do either of you remember anything odd or off from that night?" I ask.

"I remember we drank too much," Clarence says.

"Anything else?"

"Nothing that means anything," Sarah says.

"Mind telling me anyway?"

"It was just an off year," Sarah says. "Nothing big. Everyone was just sort of over it all before we ever got started good. The holidays, you know?"

"I remember Keith and Christopher checking on her a lot throughout the night," Clarence says.

"They always did," Sarah adds. "They were great parents. Very attentive. Some parents . . . well, if something happens to their child you might think . . . you know, that it was inevitable, but with parents like them . . . it's so unfair. Anyway, mind if we do this another time? We need to get everyone fed and get the search started."

DAY 95

Day 95

I'm starting to look at everyone suspiciously now.

Is this just the way it's going to be from now on?

Has my perception so shifted that I wonder what ulterior motive everyone I meet has? Will I always wonder what monster is lurking behind the masks that look like men?

Am I imagining that Wren and Brooke won't look me in the eye any longer?

Am I crazy to think that Keith and Scott are conspiring against me behind my back?

Is Vic avoiding me?

Why did Henrique leave?

Am I just paranoid? How can I know?

I'm losing my mind.

20

My phone vibrates in my pocket.

I pull it out, hoping it's Anna, back to her old self, calling to say she misses me and can't wait to see me.

Instead, it's Reggie Summers, the sheriff of Gulf County and my boss, returning my call.

"Don't tell me you've got something for me already," I say.

"I do," she says.

"That was fast."

I had texted her earlier to see if she could find any information on the Samuelsons' grandchild that died. I didn't expect anything this quickly.

"That's me," she says. "A fast woman."

"Think I read something about that in the men's restroom at the sheriff's department," I say. "Or maybe it was the jail. How are things there?"

"We're surviving," she says. "Slowly making a little progress. Look forward to having you back over here to help."

"I feel guilty not being there," I say.

"You should," she says. "So here's what I got. The Samuelsons were actually watching their grandson when he was killed. From all I can tell—based on the investigation and the media coverage—it was an accident. They were keeping him for their daughter at her place while she and her new boyfriend went to some swanky all-inclusive resort in Mexico."

"Swanky?"

"Yeah," she says, "I'm bringing it back. Soon all the kids will be using it. You watch. It'll be in rap songs and in tragic teen movie dialog. Anyway . . . The kid was five at the time. Typical toddler. Constant movement and motion. And they just both looked away at the same wrong moment. Their attention drifted way for a split second and he was gone."

"Abducted?" I ask.

"No. He fell into a swimming pool. It had a cover on it, and it wrapped around him and he took part of it down with him while the other part of it floated and prevented them from being able to get to him. By the time they did, he was already dead. They pulled him out and attempted CPR, called 911, tried everything they could, but it was no use."

"Damn."

"Yeah. Their daughter blames them and has cut them off completely."

We are quiet a moment.

"But I found something else that might be something," she says. "Seems suspicious as hell. Definitely worth a closer look. They had already lost a son several years before. That's how they got all their money. It's insurance money from the death of their son. It also looks like an accident, and maybe it is. Some families seem to have more than their fair share of tragedy, but . . ."

"How did he die?"

"Car accident," she says. "I've got a call in to the highway patrol to see if there's anything suspicious about it. I'll let you know what I find out."

.   .   .

ABOUT TWENTY OF us search a small quadrant from the grid that Brent Tremblay created.

We are no more than a few feet apart, our heads down, poking and raking the ground with the tips of our aluminum walking poles.

It's slow and tedious, which makes it all the more impressive that so many of these volunteers have done it for so long.

"How long we been doing this?" Demi Gonzalez says.

She is on my left side and she's asking Charis Tremblay who is on my right.

Derinda Dacosta, who is to Christopher's right, says, "Several months and, hey, we covered almost a postage stamp of property."

Charis laughs and says, "We've covered a little more than that. Why do you ask, Demi?"

"Do y'all find it odd that in all that time Vic Frankford has never been out here and suddenly today he is?"

"He was probably inspired by John's talk," Derinda says.

"I really enjoyed what you had to say this morning," Charis says.

"I did too," Demi adds.

"Me three," Derinda says.

"I've been volunteering at the jail near where I live in Destin for several years now," Charis says, "and I've seen firsthand how much injustice there is in our justice system."

"Thank you all," I say. "I appreciate your kind words."

"It's interesting to hear someone like you," Demi says. "When it comes to faith and religious expression it seems like most everyone I encounter is at one extreme or the other—extremely religious in a rigid, rules-based way or not religious at all. You seem to be a very smart and thoughtful person who has incorporated his practice of faith into his otherwise full life."

"That's very nice of you," I say. "It's certainly what I attempt to do, but it's a practice. One I often fail at."

"I used to be part of the rigid and rules-based crowd she's talking about," Charis says.

"Yes, you did," Demi says with a smile. "Every other word out of her mouth was Jesus and God and some damn Bible verse. Drove me crazy. But she was the best foster mom on the block."

"Sorry I was like that," she says. "Part of the reason I became a foster mom was to be able to put into practice the love and faith I was trying to live. I heard this song when I was a teenager that said don't tell them Jesus loves them until you're ready to love them too—or something like that."

"Exactly," Derinda says. "Those are great words to live by."

"And you really do," Demi says.

"I try to, but . . . like John said, I mostly fail too. I want my faith to be action instead of beliefs, practices instead of just words, but . . ."

"Like organizing this great search for my grandbaby," Derinda says.

"Maybe, but this may have more to do with guilt than grace. I feel so bad about being resistant to Keith and Christopher. Wasn't my finest hour. Probably still trying to make up for that. And I know a lot of people think it was just because they're gay, but there was more to it than that. I just wanted Magdalene to have a mother."

"We can all understand that," Derinda says.

"But as I got to know Keith and Christopher, I realized a mother's love doesn't just come from females."

"That's so true," Demi says. "It's obvious John has a father and a mother's love for little Taylor."

I start to say something, but stop as a volunteer to my far

left begins yelling. "I got something. I got something. Over here. Over here."

Someone to our right blows a whistle.

"Everyone freeze," Keith yells. "Please. Don't move. Anyone."

Every volunteer stops in place.

"It's . . . it's . . . I think it's her pajamas."

"Who is that?" Derinda asks. "Whose voice is that?"

"Vic Frankford's," Demi says. "First day searching with us and he finds her pajamas. That's not suspicious at all."

DAY 104

Day 104

I thought Henrique had abandoned us. I really did. He just vanished after what happened. No goodbye, no explanation, but now he's back. And sadly he's confirmed what we all have suspected for a while. He's sick and the prognosis is not good. It's not as tragic as if he were a young man (or a young girl who was just starting her life), but it is sad nonetheless. He's not old-old. All of us hope to live to be older than what he is now, and despite everything I still hope that for Magdalene—and a small part of me still holds out hope that she might get to. But that part of me is shrinking by the day.

21

"Why're you so certain these are hers?" Roderick Brandt asks.

He's a forty-something white man with pale skin and dark hair. Not fat, but far heavier and softer than I'd expect someone in his position to be. He looks more like a cell phone salesman than a cop—especially in his light blue cotton button-down that blouses above his belt and the too-long burgundy Sears and Roebuck tie around his neck.

A few moments after Vic Frankford found the pj's, the Walton County Sheriff's Department was called and everyone involved in the search slowly turned and walked back out of the woods in as close to the same way we came in as we could.

When Roderick arrived—which he did alone, no crime scene investigators or anyone else—he asked me to take him to the spot where the pj's were discovered and were still lying.

"Shouldn't I take you, Detective?" Vic Frankford had said. "I was the one to find them after all."

His darkly dyed hair, which starts about halfway up his head, is short and fro-like and doesn't move as he does—not even in the breeze. Beneath it his black eyes, which never quite make full contact, are hard and kind of vacant.

"Just hang around," Roderick had responded. "I'll get your statement when I get back and have a better idea of what we're dealing with."

Now, Roderick and I are kneeling down next to the pajamas, black Nitrile gloves on our hands, disposable white Tyvek shoe covers on our feet.

"I know she was supposed to be wearing a pair of these when she went missing," he is saying, "but why are you so certain these are hers?"

"Dolly Parton Hard Candy Apple Red Christmas nail polish," I say.

"Say what?"

I explain it to him.

"Okay," he says, nodding, "that's pretty damn convincing. So let's say that you're right and these actually *are* the pajamas Magdalene Dacosta was wearing when she was abducted, why do they look, apart from the polish stain, nearly brand new?"

"I have no idea," I say.

"They're not even really dirty," he says, "let alone deteriorating. No way they've been out here since she's been missing."

"No, they haven't."

"We're talkin' ten months."

I nod.

"And if they haven't been out there," he says. "Where have they been? And why aren't they on her and why were they taken off? And as long as I'm asking . . . Where the hell is she?"

"Her room has been left the way it was—besides what forensics did," I say, "so we should be able to get DNA from something of hers, a hairbrush or something, and compare it to make certain these are hers. I know it was collected during the original investigation but I'd like to do it again for comparison.

I'd like to do everything that we can again—as if we're investigating this case for the first time."

He nods. "Absolutely," he says. "I have no problem with that. I was just one of the investigators involved and I had some questions about the work some of the others did—especially after hearing some of their homophobic comments. But assuming they are her pajamas—and that's what I'm assuming —we need to get the FDLE crime scene unit out here to process these and search for . . . what else might be out here."

I nod.

"But we both agree that these are probably hers, right?" he says.

I nod again. "I think there's a good chance they are."

"And that they haven't been out here for the past ten months."

"Right."

"You have any ideas on why her abductor would keep these somewhere else all this time and then dump them out here now?"

I frown and shake my head. "Not really. Nothing that wouldn't be wild conjecture with no evidence to support it."

"Well, let's see if we can't find some evidence and figure out what the hell is going on."

"Won't get any arguments from me," I say.

"And another thing," he says. "Look at how these are . . . I don't know . . . displayed or whatever. Didn't bother to hide them, did they?"

"Somebody wanted them found."

"And feel that . . ." He lifts a corner of them with his gloved hand and I reach over and feel it with my gloved hand. "Bone dry," he says. "That dry and that clean. They're soft, not stiff at all. If they had been out here a day or more, wouldn't getting wet from rain or even dew and then drying out in the sun make them stiff?"

I nod. "Almost seems like they were dropped out here today," I say.

"That's what I'm thinking," he says. "And maybe by the man who was supposed to have found them."

Day III

There is no pain, no misery, no agony, no suffering like losing a child. None. Absolutely none. Nothing compares to this. Not even losing Keith would be as unbearable as this. I want to die every second of every day just to have this constant ache and heartbreak end. It's with me every moment of every day, this unimaginable loss. There's never a breath, never a single second that this acute agony isn't my constant companion.

22

Many of the volunteers have joined Keith and Christopher, their friends and family at the Florida House. Most of the people who were in the house the night Magdalene was taken are present. Even Scott Haskew and Jodi North, who didn't participate in the search, are here. As is Henrique Arango, whose failing health prevents him from such physical exertion. Of those who participated in the search but are now absent are Demi Gonzalez and, the man of the hour who discovered the Toy Story pajamas, Vic Frankford.

Most everyone is in the hallway, parlor, or dining room.

Charis had served tea and coffee as everyone arrived and is now going around offering refills. Clarence and Sarah had brought the leftovers from the search and had one of their staff members meet them here with more food—all of which, seemingly untouched, is spread out across the enormous dining table.

When I walk in they stop talking and look at me expectantly, as if I have come to deliver the update they've been waiting on.

Keith and Christopher are on one of the couches in the parlor, Derinda between them with an arm around each.

"Are they . . . hers?" Christopher asks.

"We can't know for sure yet," I say, "but based on what you've told me I'd say it's at least possible. But there are many questions. We can't be sure of anything yet. We'll know more after they've been processed and a DNA comparison has been conducted. I'm very sorry, but none of it will be fast."

Wren Melody, who is sitting next to Brooke Wakefield on an ornate red velvet loveseat that appears to be an antique, says, "Surely you can give them more than that, pet."

From a folding chair across the room, Rake Sabin says, "I don't think he was finished."

"FDLE is being called in," I continue. "My guess is they will not only process the pajamas but search that area and, if the Walton County sheriff requests it, provide an investigator— maybe more than one. But it's the sheriff's call. It's his department's investigation. Not only do I have nothing to do with it, but even Roderick won't get to make most of the decisions— and it's his case. There will be a lot more waiting involved. Chances are nothing will happen particularly quickly, but just know that a lot will be happening—as much or more than when she first went missing."

"Any chance you could share with us any of the 'many questions' about what was found?" Henrique asks.

He is slumped in a high-back chair near the dark, unused fireplace.

I shake my head. "I know how frustrating it is," I say, "and I'm sorry. There really are good reasons for withholding information in an investigation, but at this time I just don't know anything with enough certainty to do anything but speculate."

"We understand," Keith says. "Will you still keep looking into it?"

"I can if you want me to, but you really don't need me to

now that the Walton County Sheriff's Department and FDLE are taking a more active role."

"What is FDLE?" Derinda asks.

"It stands for Florida Department of Law Enforcement," I say. "It's a state agency—our version of state cops. They conduct state-level investigations, but also assist smaller local law enforcement agencies in their investigations. They have specially trained investigators and a crime scene unit, and the best forensics lab in the state."

"And they're taking over the case?" she asks.

"No," I say. "They don't take over cases. They will assist Walton County—only do what they ask them to."

"I'd feel better if you continued investigating it for us," she says.

"Me too," Keith says.

"Yeah," Christopher adds. "Absolutely."

"I'd be happy to do what I can, but it will be in the background—like it has been, only more so. And chances are they won't share any information with me, so I won't know anything you won't. And it will probably be from afar. Given this new development, I figured you'd want to postpone the other talks for this week and focus on—"

From a dining table chair in the entryway between the dining room and the parlor, Scott Haskew clears his throat and says, "That's probably a good idea. We could reschedule for another time—perhaps in the spring."

"Just make sure it doesn't conflict with our spring art series and theater camp," Jodi North says.

"Even if we do postpone the rest of the talks, which I hate to do," Christopher says, "would you lead a prayer vigil for Magdalene and maybe say a few things about her?"

I nod. "Sure," I say. "I'd be honored."

"I hope this goes without saying," Keith says, "but you and

your family are more than welcome stay here as long as you like—not just while you're giving the talks or working the case."

"Thank you," I say, "that's—"

The buzzer sounds indicating someone is out front, and Rake Sabin tells Keith and Christopher he'll take care of it and for them to keep their seats.

"Maybe it's the police with some news for us," Derinda says.

Not likely, I think but don't say.

"What the hell?" Rake says as he looks on the screen behind the check-in desk.

"What is it?" Keith asks.

"I can't believe it," Rake says. "It's . . . it's . . . it's Hal Raphael."

Rake presses the button that pops the lock on the front door and a few moments later Hal Raphael walks in carrying a suitcase.

It is surreal to see him just walk in like this, suitcase in hand. Evidently, I'm not the only one who feels this way.

The gathered crowd considers the intruding stranger with equal parts surprise and suspicion.

It's as if everyone is asking themselves the same question: *Is this a case of the criminal returning to the scene of crime?*

Sort of bowing as he enters the room, he says, "Hello, everyone. Keith. Christopher. I was back in the area on business and I wanted to stop in and see how you were and when I heard about the searches y'all are doing, I wanted to see if I could help. Do you happen to have a vacant room available?"

Keith glances at me and I nod.

"Sure," he says. "We'll find a place for you. And I think our investigator would like to ask you to some questions."

"Sure," Raphael says. "Anything I can do. I'm here to help. I would've come sooner, but . . . There's really no other way to say it but that fate prevented it. Hopefully, it's because this will wind up being a better time for my visit."

23

Back in the room, I tell Anna about the day's developments.

She seems uninterested and a bit bored.

Usually, she listens attentively and asks insightful questions about the cases I'm working on, but in this moment I'm not sure she's hearing me at all.

"Given all that," I say, "especially Hal being back, I don't think it's a good idea for Taylor to be here. Had I known more about the case from the beginning I don't think I would've brought her. With what I know now and with all that is happening . . ."

"Wait, you've put my daughter in danger by having us here?"

"I just want to make sure she's not," I say. "Magdalene's disappearance feels like a one-off more than part of a series being done by a compulsive criminal, but I can't be certain."

She pushes herself off the bed and begins to gather things. "Then let's go then. Help me pack our things."

"They've asked me to lead a prayer service for Magdalene," I say. "And to continue investigating the case even though they're going to postpone the rest of the talks until the spring."

"So what are you saying?" she says. "You don't want us to go? Oh, wait, you want to just send me and Taylor away?"

"No," I say. "Not at all."

"That's exactly it," she says. "You're tryin' to get rid of us."

"Anna," I say, my voice firm. "Listen to yourself. Can you not hear how extreme and unreasonable you're being?"

"Oh, *I'm* the one being extreme and unreasonable?" she says.

"Yes," I say. "You are. I love you. I'm here for you. That's not going to change. But you have changed. It's like you're someone else entirely. I want you to go have a physical and just see if—"

"I don't need a fuckin' physical. Just tell me what you were sayin' if you weren't sayin' you wanted to stay and send us away."

"My first priority is Taylor's safety," I say. "As much as I want to try to help find Magdalene, I'd gladly give that up to protect Taylor. If you'll recall, I'm the one who brought this up. I was suggesting that we leave. Not just you and Taylor. All three of us. But I was letting you know that I'd like to come back to lead the prayer service for Magdalene and help with the investigation some when I can."

"Sure you were," she says. "When is the prayer service thing?"

"In the morning."

"And you were going to go home with us and then drive all the way back out here in the morning to do the service?"

"That was my plan. I brought up the prayer service and continuing to help with the investigation to see if you'd have a problem with me coming back some—maybe even every day this week since I'm already off work."

"So Taylor and I don't get a vacation, but you get to keep playin' detective?"

"I don't actually *play* detective," I say. "I *am* one—which is how I was able to detect the subtle changes in you recently."

"Cute," she says.

"It was mean and I shouldn't've said it. I'm sorry."

"Do you have your gun?" she asks.

"Anna, I'm not going to just let you shoot me."

Without responding to what I said, she says, "Where is your weapon?"

"One is locked in the glove compartment," I say. "And one is in my holster. Why?"

"I was just making sure you had one," she says. "Magdalene was taken while she was alone in her room and her parents were in the other end of this huge house, right?"

I nod.

"We're not going to leave Taylor alone for even a moment and you have a weapon," she says. "There's no need for us to leave tonight. We'll stay tonight. You can do the service in the morning and work on the case some tomorrow while Taylor and I enjoy a little more time at the beach, and then we'll go. She can sleep between us in our bed. No one's breaking in here tonight and taking her from us."

It's the most reasoned and reasonable argument she's made in two weeks.

"Okay," I say. "The reason my Glock is locked in the car is that it doesn't have a safety. The Smith that I have on me does. I'll leave the safety on but have it on the bedside table next to me."

"That's fine," she says, "but you won't need it. Someone comes in here to do harm to my little girl and I will rip them apart with my teeth."

24

"How are y'all feeling?" I ask.

It's my first chance to speak with Keith and Christopher by themselves.

We are in the kitchen of their residence. It's quiet back here. The front part of the Florida House is still filled with friends and family hoping to get more information tonight.

"I feel so many different things," Christopher says. "None of them good."

Keith nods. "Yeah, it's like we've wanted something—anything—all this time, but this . . . It just raises more questions and doesn't give us any answers or comfort."

"*Comfort*?" Christopher says. "Just the opposite."

Derinda walks in pushing a hotel-style cleaning cart and tells Keith she's finished with Raphael's room. "I don't like having him here in this house," she says. "Don't like it at all."

Keith nods to her, and she pushes the cart into the supply closet along the far wall as Christopher continues.

"Why did he take her pajamas off? We know why, don't we? And it had to be so quick after he took her."

Derinda joins us at the table, pulling her chair over

between her son and his husband and placing a supportive, comforting hand on each man. She is clearly distressed, and it is obvious that she has been broken by this entire ordeal—both as a mother and a grandmother.

"What did our poor little girl go through?" Christopher is saying, his gaze in the distance seeing nothing now present in this room. "Is her naked little body buried out there too? Is there anything left of it? Oh my God."

He breaks down and begins to sob, and we all have tears in our eyes.

I wait for a moment while Derinda and Keith attempt to comfort him and each other.

"I understand how difficult it is to do," I say, "but if at all possible . . . if you could just wait a little longer and try not to draw any inferences from anything yet . . . I know it's nearly impossible, but the truth is we don't know for sure that those *are* Magdalene's pajamas."

"Who else's could they *be*?" Christopher says.

"And even if they are," I say, "we don't know what that means. There's a lot that doesn't make sense about what was found today. We just don't know anything yet."

Brooke Wakefield and Charis Tremblay appear in the doorway.

Though they aren't crying at the moment, their eyes are puffy and red, their faces stricken—especially Charis's.

"So sorry to interrupt," Brooke says, "but . . . Rake is insisting on staying here tonight. Says with Raphael back in the house he wants to be around to help if anything happens."

"I think it's a good idea," Charis says.

"He's gone to pack a bag and grab his toothbrush," Brooke says. "He said he'd just stay on the couch because he doesn't plan on sleeping much anyway, but I wanted to see if there's a room he can use—maybe one next to Raphael's—and Charis offered to get it ready for him so none of you would have to."

"That's so sweet of all three of you," Derinda says.

Keith nods and says, "I like the idea of having his muscles here. Let's put him in five. It's right across from Raphael's room."

Christopher nods.

My phone vibrates. I pull it out of my pocket and glance at it.

"It's Roderick," I say. "Mind if I take it?"

They all nod.

"Please," Keith says.

I answer it, and as I do they all whisper about getting Rake's room ready, and Brooke and Charis rush off to take care of it.

"Where are you?" Roderick asks.

I tell him.

"Can you meet a little later tonight?"

"Sure."

"How would you feel about working this case with me?" he asks.

"What do you mean?"

"I mean my sheriff called yours and they worked it out," Roderick is saying. "My sheriff asked me if I wanted an FDLE investigator on this and I told him I'd rather have you and he said he'd see what he could do."

"Oh wow, well thank you," I say. "I'm very flattered. And I'd be honored . . ."

"But?"

I explain to him about my concerns for Taylor and my plan to take her home. As I do, Keith, Christopher, and Derinda react to what I'm saying with a mixture of surprise and sadness.

"Ah, man, I didn't even think about that," Roderick says. "I was looking forward to working this thing with you but I get it. I'd do the same thing with my daughter. Let me give it some thought and see if we might come up with a solution—would that be okay? Maybe we could post a deputy there or find y'all another place to stay. I don't know. Something. You still up for meeting with me later tonight? Could we talk about it more then?"

"Absolutely."

When I disconnect the call, Keith says, "I can't believe we didn't even think about the possibility that the same thing could happen to your daughter. I'm so sorry."

"We're selfish and self-centered people," Christopher says. "Only think about ourselves. Here you are helping us and we didn't even realize by doing so you were putting your daughter in harm's way."

"I might not be," I say. "We just can't know for sure yet. It's possible that what happened to Magdalene was specific to her, but if it wasn't . . ."

"It'd be a little bit of a drive for y'all and the accommodations aren't nearly as nice," Derinda says, "but y'all are more than welcome to stay with me."

"Thank you," I say. "That's so generous of you."

"You're trying to find my only grandchild," she says. "I'd say it's the very least I could do. It's killing me to see what my boys are going through. If we could just get her back . . ."

"Roderick just mentioned the possibility of having a deputy posted here or finding us another place to stay, but I think my wife has decided she really just wants to get back home."

"I certainly understand that," Derinda says. "We all wish we had taken Magdalene far, far from here before she was . . ."

"I hate to sound like the selfish asshole that I am," Keith says, "but does that mean you won't be able to work on finding out what happened to Magdalene?"

"No, I'll still do what I can," I say. "I'll take the casebook y'all made me and do what I am able to from over there and come back over here as I can."

"Again, I hate to be the asshole," Keith says, "but did Officer Brandt have any news?"

I shake my head. "Not that he shared, but we're supposed to meet later tonight. I'll let you know anything I find out."

"You've done so much for us," Keith says. "We're so grateful."

Christopher, who is looking off into the distance, says, "Our home isn't safe for children . . . for little girls . . . for sweet little Taylor."

25

As I'm coming out of our room from checking on Anna and Taylor again—something I find myself doing every few minutes—I see Rake Sabin coming up the stairs with a gym bag in his right hand, its contents causing the muscles in his flexing arm to bulge against his tight athletic T.

"Hey, John," he says when he sees me. "I want you to know that I'll be keeping an eye on your room tonight too."

"Thank you."

"Rest easy and get some good sleep," he says. "I got this. I appreciate all you're doing—the inspiring talks and helping to find out what happened to little Magdalene. I know that's a lot on you, so just don't worry about your family tonight. They're safe."

"I really appreciate that," I say.

He nods toward Hal Raphael's door. "Can you believe the balls on this bastard? Walking in here like he owns the place, demanding a room, acting as if we don't all believe he's the one responsible for what happened. Wonder why he's back? Why now?"

"I hope we can find out."

Charis opens the door of Rake's room and steps out on the landing with us. "You're all ready," she says. "Not my best work, but probably my quickest."

"I just appreciate you doing it," Rake says. "But you really needn't have bothered. I won't be sleeping—or even using the room much for that matter. But thank you just the same."

"Pleasure," she says.

"Well, I'm gonna go grab a quick shower so I can be fresh and alert the rest of the night," he says, and disappears into his room.

"That was very nice of you to do," I say.

She shrugs. "It was nothing. Besides, it helps keep my mind off . . . other things—like what the Frankford man found and . . . things like that."

I nod. "I know everyone around here focuses on Keith and Christopher's loss and grief, but yours has to be very similar."

Tears appear in her eyes and she nods. "They only had her a little longer than I did," she says. "And part of me will always feel like her mother. Can I tell you something in confidence? I need to tell someone and . . . there's no one else around here I can tell."

I nod. "Of course."

"I genuinely love Keith and Christopher," she says. "It took me longer to come around than it should have, but . . . I got there eventually. I just got to thinking—I mean back when Demi told me they were planning to adopt Magdalene—there's no couple who could adopt her that I would agree with everything about them. I just needed to know that they would love her and take good care of her no matter what. I'm a work in progress."

"We all are," I say.

"And I'm not saying I agree with gay marriage or whatever, but I could see that they both had a lot of love to give and they planned to give it to her. That was good enough for me. I mean,

I still wanted her to have a mother, but . . . I've fostered a lot of kids over the years and I've learned that the thing that matters most is finding them a good placement where they will be loved and cared for. There are no perfect people or places, but . . . a good one is good enough. As you can imagine I've wanted to keep nearly all the children I've fostered over the years, but some of them—like Magdalene—have an even more special place in my heart. And they always will. So yes, she still feels like mine. I feel like her mother."

I nod and give her an understanding look. I genuinely feel for her—more so because of how much I'm missing Johanna.

"Here's the secret I'm keeping that I need to tell someone . . ." she says. "As much as I love and care about Keith and Christopher, and as much as what I'm doing to help I'm doing for them, I'm doing it far more for Magdalene. And if . . . I know this is a very big if and isn't likely, but if . . . we somehow find her alive . . . I plan to sue for custody, to . . . try to adopt her myself. And it's not because Keith and Christopher are gay. It's because they didn't protect her. They didn't keep her safe. And maybe it's just because their home is like this public house with strangers coming and going or maybe it was that party and all the drinking and whatever else went on, but . . . they left that sweet little angel vulnerable somehow and I just can't stand by without trying to stop that from happening again. It's nothing against them, and I realize that chances are I will lose, but I have to try. I have to. I get that it could've happened to anyone, but as much as I care for them my first responsibility is to Magdalene. Do you understand that at all?"

"I do," I say. "Of course. Keeping my children safe is more important to me than anything else. I feel like it's my first responsibility, so I certainly understand."

"I know the chances of getting her back alive are . . . minuscule, which breaks my heart. The only thing that breaks it more is her being alive out there somewhere and being abused and tortured. Anyway, it's a very long shot and even if it happens, no judge is ever going to give me custody. I know that. And I know that I will lose them as friends—them and Derinda and probably even Demi, but I'm hoping that by trying it will inspire Keith and Christopher to be better, more cautious parents. I'd rather try and fail than not try at all. I'd rather lose them as friends and risk never seeing her again if it means she'll be safe then . . . Please tell me you understand—at least a little."

"I do," I say, nodding, my eyes locked onto hers, which have tears in them.

"And please don't tell anyone. I want to be able to keep helping, to stay close, to be a part of everything that is being done for her. We've formed a kind of family and I'd be devastated if I lost that too."

"I understand," I say.

"I feel so much better having told you but now I'm scared you'll tell them."

"I won't," I say.

"Oh, thank you," she says, and steps forward and hugs me. "Thank you so much."

26

A s Charis and I reach the first floor, we find that no one has left, and that the group has been joined by Vic Frankford.

"I don't know," he is saying. "I really don't. I've never been before, but I don't know, something just kept telling me to go today."

Evidently, he is regaling everyone with how he found the Toy Story pajamas in the woods. Equally evident is that it's not a short story.

We remain standing in the foyer close to the staircase. Though Taylor and Anna are safely locked inside our room and Anna is completely capable of protecting Taylor, I want to be as close as possible to them as I can, and from here I can keep an eye on the front door and the stairs too. No one can even get to our room door without me knowing—much less inside the room itself.

"It's not easy for me to get away from my market," he says. "God knows I would've liked to have gone on the searches before now, but . . . my customers expect to find me when they come into my store."

Most of his customers are tourists who don't know him or that he is the owner.

"And I owe it to them to be there," he says. "But I was here that night—the night little Magdalene was taken from us—and I owe something to her too. And to my dear friends, her parents. So I said to myself, I'm going today and all the rest can rot. And good thing I did, I can tell you that."

He says it as if he hadn't been there the pajamas wouldn't have been found. But if he hadn't been there someone else would've walked his line. Even with him there, a few feet in either direction and the person next to him would have found it.

"I try to listen to that little voice inside my head," he is saying. "It has never led me astray. It's a tiny whisper most of the time, but when I hear it I do my best to honor it by doing what it is telling me to do."

"What exactly did it tell you to do?" Henrique asks, and it's obvious he's having some fun at Vic's expense. "Did it give you the coordinates of the garment?"

"No, nothing like that," Vic says, and it's equally as obvious that he is oblivious to what is happening. "It's very subtle. Like an impression. A feeling."

"A thought?" Henrique offers.

"Sure, yeah. Like that. The thing is, it's easy to miss."

"Many things in this world are," Henrique says with a smile.

During my last visit to our room upstairs, Anna had informed me that she had called her dad and he would be picking up her and Taylor in the morning, and that since they wouldn't be home for a while anyway, I should stay to work the case with Roderick. I tried to talk her into reconsidering and us just going home, but she was adamant that she and Taylor were going to her parents' place in Dothan and that the time apart would do us good.

As the others are talking, I text Roderick and let him know I can work the case with him if he still wants me.

Hell yeah, I still want you to, he had responded. *That's great news. I'm five minutes away. I'll brief the family and then we can meet. And I'm bringing a deputy to stay there tonight for extra security.*

"I hate to leave good company," Derinda says, "but this ol' gal can't hang like she used'a could."

"Investigator Brandt is on his way," I say.

"He's been on his way for hours now," she says. "Besides, just like you, he ain't gonna tell us anything anyway. 'Course, if I'm wrong and he does, call me immediately. If not, I'll be back over in the morning and y'all can tell me what he didn't tell you then."

"You sure you don't want to stay here tonight?" Keith asks.

She shakes her head. "Hard enough just coming in here. I could never sleep here."

"Text us when you get home safe," Christopher says.

"Will do," she says. "And thank you all again for all y'all are doing for Magdalene and our family."

"I'll walk you out," Henrique says, slowly pushing himself up. "I too can hear my own bed calling."

Beside me, Charis yawns. "Sounds like you're ready for your bed too," I say.

"That may be," she says, "but wild, wild horses couldn't drag me away from here tonight. I have to hear what Mr. Brandt says."

"It has to be him, doesn't it?" Vic Frankford is saying.

He's looking up at the ceiling, and it's clear he's talking about Hal Raphael.

"I mean, if it's not," he continues, "it's one of us, and there's no way it's one of us."

"It's him," Clarence Samuelson says. "I can't believe he's back here. Can't believe y'all are letting him stay here."

"If it's him," Keith says, "this is exactly where we want him to be."

"I feel like between us, we could get him to confess," Clarence says.

Keith glances over at me. I shake my head.

"For now, let's wait to see what Roderick has to say," Keith says.

"It's not just that a coerced confession wouldn't be admissible in court," I say. "It's that you can't trust them. Apply the right amount of torture and you can get anybody to say anything."

Christopher nods vigorously.

"I get it," Clarence says. "It's just hard to do nothing."

"Things are happening," I say. "We have a potentially hugely significant clue. It just takes time. And lots of it. I know how trying it can be, but unfortunately there's no way around it, no shortcut that leads to anything good."

"It's not anything good I want it to lead to," Clarence says.

"By *good* I meant anything approximating justice."

A little while later, the front door buzzer sounds and several people jump.

Keith steps over behind the desk and looks at the monitor. "It's Roderick," he says as he buzzes him in.

oderick Brandt, looking exhausted and on edge, enters the room with a female deputy named Haskins.

She is a tall, large woman with a blond ponytail and a pale, puffy face with roundish, red smudges like natural rouge on her cheeks.

Christopher stands and Keith moves back over to stand beside him, putting his arm around him as he does.

"Y'all look like you could use some food and something to drink," Charis says to the two cops. "What can I get you?"

"Got any coffee?" Roderick asks.

"Just made a fresh pot," she says, and crosses the room to get it. "Two coffees coming up."

"You sure we can't get you anything to eat?" Sarah Samuelson asks. "We have a lot of different things and a ton of it."

Roderick glances at Haskins.

She nods and says, "I missed dinner."

"Well, go help yourself," he says. "Everybody, this is Deputy

Haskins." He looks over at Keith and Christopher. "If it's okay with y'all I'd like her to stay here tonight."

"*Okay?*" Keith says. "You kiddin'? We'd love to have her."

"Welcome," Christopher says to her.

Sarah takes Haskins into the dining room and begins to uncover the various dishes. "Have a seat and just tell me what you'd like. I'll fix your plate."

Rake Sabin comes down the stairs and into the parlor. "Everything's quiet up there," he says. "Just gonna grab a cup of coffee and head back up to keep watch."

Roderick shoots me a quizzical look. "Hal Raphael showed up tonight. He's in a room upstairs."

"What?"

"Rake's keeping an eye on his room," I say.

Charis hands Haskins a cup of coffee and points to the cream and sugar on the table, then brings Brandt's back into the parlor.

"Cream or sugar?" she asks.

"Just black, thanks."

He takes the coffee and sips it.

Everyone in the room is looking at him expectantly.

"Come on, Rake," Charis says, "let's get you taken care of. Would you like some food?"

She leads him into the dining room.

Roderick looks at Keith and Christopher and says, "There somewhere we could talk?"

"Here is fine," Christopher says. "We'd tell them what you said afterward anyway, so . . ."

Roderick nods and takes another sip of his coffee. "Mind if we sit down?"

"Of course not, sorry," Christopher says. "Sit here."

He indicates a chair next to the couch he and Keith had been on before and the three men take a seat.

"Obviously, there's not much I can tell you at this point," Roderick says, "but I wanted to come by and give you an update so you know what's going on. We called in FDLE and their crime scene has processed the scene, but they're coming back out in the morning to extend it outwards and start a more thorough search of the area. The pajamas have been taken to their lab for processing. In the morning a team will come by and process Magdalene's room for DNA samples again to compare to the pajamas we found."

"But they already did that," Keith says. "Don't you still have her DNA on file?"

Roderick nods. "We do. And we will compare it too, but we're going to retest it as well."

"Do you think they're hers?" Christopher asks. "They have to be, right?"

"Honestly, we just don't know," he says. "They match the description of what she was wearing that night, but . . . they look relatively new. They certainly haven't been out there in the elements since Magdalene was abducted, so . . ."

"That's good, right?" Christopher says. "Means she's alive."

"The truth is we have no idea what it means. If they are hers, then it doesn't make any sense at all. Like I said, it's just too early to tell. The good news is FDLE has a great lab and they've agreed to rush everything for us. We could know something as soon as tomorrow afternoon. Then we can work on what it means. For now, try to get some rest. Sleep will help you more than anything to cope with whatever we face the next few days."

They both nod, but Christopher says, "I'll never be able to sleep tonight."

"The other thing I wanted you to know is that our sheriff has okayed it with the Gulf County sheriff for John to work with me on this."

They look over at me in surprise. I nod.

"That's great," Keith says.

"We're gonna do everything we can do," Roderick says. "And we're going to do it as quickly as we can, but it's not going to be fast. I know you're frustrated and I'm afraid you've got a lot more of that coming, but just know that all of us—me, John, our department, FDLE—all of us will be giving it our all."

"Why would they take her pajamas off?" Christopher says. "Why now? Why leave them out there like that? Has she been somewhere close by all this time?"

"Hopefully, we'll be able to find answers to all those questions and much more," Roderick says.

"Our poor little baby," Christopher says. "Is she somewhere close by right now? What's she wearing? Is she cold? Hungry? Hurt?"

Continuing to rub Christopher's back, Keith looks at Roderick. "Shouldn't we be out there looking for her right now? Why are they waiting until morning to—"

From up in our room Anna begins screaming frantically. Between shrieks she yells for Taylor and for me.

I turn and begin running toward the screams.

Dropping his coffee and following me, Roderick yells, "Everyone stay here. Haskins, keep them here!"

28

O ur room door is closed and locked, and I use my key
card to get in.

I fling open the door to find Anna alone,
searching for Taylor.

"Do you have her?" she yells. "Is she with you?"

"No. She was here just a few minutes ago when I checked
on y'all."

"I woke up to find her gone."

I turn to Roderick. "Can you and Haskins cover the doors to
make sure nobody leaves while we look for her inside?"

"Yeah," he says, turning to leave immediately. "I'll call for
backup. As soon as they get here I'll be back in to help search
the house."

He starts running toward the stairs but I call after him.

He pauses and turns back toward me.

Behind me, Anna is calling out for Taylor and continuing to
search the room.

"Check the security camera feeds first," I say. "Make sure
she hasn't already been taken from the house. You can still see

the front door from the check-in desk where they are, so you can watch it and scan the footage at the same time."

"Got it," he says, and takes off again.

When I turn back toward Anna, she is on her hands and knees looking under the bed.

I rush into the bathroom and look around, opening the cabinet doors under the sink and pulling back the shower curtain.

I run back into the room and open the door to the small closet. I then pull up the top of the unzipped suitcase on the aluminum luggage rack, and as I do a thought tries to form but is quickly gone.

"I've already looked in there," Anna says. "I've looked everywhere. She's not here."

"I'm just double-checking," I say. "I'm gonna go over every inch of the house this way."

"I can't believe you let this happen," she says.

I don't respond. Instead, I open and look inside each drawer of the dresser.

As I do, my phone vibrates. I pull it out and see that it's Roderick and answer it.

"Somebody disabled the recorder," he says. "The cameras are still hooked up but they haven't been recording since earlier tonight. We have no way of knowing if she's already out of the house or not."

I slam my hand down on the dresser as expletives explode from my mouth.

"I've got roadblocks being set up on the three roads out of here and backup should be here in about two more minutes. Everybody down here wants to help. Keith called his mom and she is headed back, but he hasn't been able to get Henrique yet. Everyone is down here with me except you, Anna, and Haskins, who is on the back door."

"And Hal Raphael," I say, stepping to the landing and looking at his door. "Who even with all the screams and commotion hasn't even opened his door to see what's going on?"

I step across the landing and begin banging on Raphael's door.

After getting no response from calling for him and beating on the door, I step back and kick it near the handle.

I could run downstairs and get a key from Keith, but not only do I not want to waste that much time, if Raphael has his door bolted it wouldn't do any good anyway.

At the first kick the door gives a little and begins to splinter, but it is not until the third one that the door swings open and slams into the wall behind it.

The room is dark and cool, and I can hear heavy snoring.

I flip on the lights and see that Raphael appears sound asleep in his bed. I do a quick sweep of the room to ensure no one else is in here, then try to wake him up.

No amount of shaking him does any good, but as I yell for him to wake up while slapping his face some, he begins to rouse.

His eyes open a little then close again. Several times.

He's either extremely groggy or an immensely talented actor.

It takes a little while and some water from the tap, but I manage to wake him and get him to sit up.

"What . . . What's going on? What is it?"

I tell him and ask him where Taylor is.

"Huh?" he says. "Who?"

"My daughter," I say. "The little girl in the room across the hallway."

"I . . . I have no idea. I took a sleeping pill and have been asleep since my head hit the pillow—just a few moments after coming into my room. I have no idea what's happening. I . . . I can't . . . even hold my eyes open."

29

Anna, Raphael, and I have joined everyone else in the parlor.

Anna is dressed—something she must have done when I was talking to Raphael. Raphael is still in his pajamas.

The room is filled with tension and adrenaline-fueled excitement that hums like electricity running along a transmission line.

The buzzer sounds and after a quick glance Roderick buzzes the front door open.

Derinda, Henrique, and two deputies rush in.

"Oh, John, I'm so sorry," Derinda says. "This can't be happening again. It's . . . it's too much."

"The deputies searched us and our car," Henrique says. "I told them we left together and everyone saw us, and we didn't have a little girl with us, but . . ."

"Search everything we have," Derinda says. "Hell, you can strip search me if you want. Just find Taylor fast."

"I want one of you in here," Roderick is saying to the deputies. "One outside on the front door. And the other four searching the neighborhood and going door to door."

One deputy stays and one turns to leave.

"And you and Haskins watch the side yards too, not just the front and back doors," Roderick says to the exiting deputy.

"You got it," he says, and is gone.

"How can we help?" Rake asks.

"I know you all want to help," Roderick says, "but the biggest help you can be right now is by staying here so we know where everybody is."

He turns to me.

"Let's form two search teams so we can get through the entire house faster," I say. "Be thorough. Check every room, every space inside every room. Everything. Keith and Christopher, do you each have a master key that works on every door in the house?"

They nod.

"Would you each go with one of the search teams, unlock every door and lead us methodically through the entire house?"

They nod again.

Christopher says, "Absolutely."

"Of course," Keith says.

"Why do you think she's still in the house?" Anna asks me.

"We can't be sure that she is," I say, "but no one has left— except Henrique and Derinda earlier, and we all saw them and know they didn't have her—and it doesn't seem like there's been enough time to get her out."

"We've got roadblocks set up," Roderick says. "And deputies in the yard and going around the neighborhood."

"Somebody needs to search the woods behind the house," Vic says. "Don't forget that's where I found the pajamas today."

"I'll lead a team out there," Anna says, her voice conveying her anger and sadness and frustration and fatigue. "I just feel like she's not in the house any longer. Do y'all have some bright flashlights?"

When I turn toward Anna and start to say something she narrows her eyes and shakes her head, her expression forbidding me from saying anything to her.

"It's dark and dangerous out there," Roderick says. "We should—"

"We're talking about my little girl," Anna says. "There's no place too dark or too dangerous. And there's nobody who's gonna stop me."

"Why not let the two deputies guarding the doors go with her?" Derinda says. "And we can watch the doors. You can put two or three of us on each door so we can watch the doors and each other. That way everything is watched and searched and everyone is accounted for."

Roderick nods. "I like that. That's a great idea."

"Just put this sleepy ass bastard in my group," Rake says, nodding toward Raphael, who is slumped in the high-back chair by the fireplace dozing. I ain't buyin' his Sleeping Beauty alibi."

DAY 173

Day 173

I've given up on understanding people. I really have. What makes them say the things they say? It has to be because of the things they think, but why would people be thinking these things? And even if they were, why would they say them? Today Brooke told me that we could just adopt again. That it wasn't like losing our own child. We had only had her for a short time and losing her wasn't the same as if we had given birth to her or had raised her her entire life. She went on to ask if we knew she was well taken care of and in good hands and happy, couldn't we just adopt again and be just as happy as we were before. I was speechless. I literally couldn't respond. It's like my little girl is replaceable, like we can just plug another child into her spot and be fine about it. What the actual fuck? How could she ask me something like that?

30

With Brooke, Wren, Derinda, and Vic watching the back door and Clarence, Sarah, Charis, Rake, Henrique, and Raphael watching the front door, Keith and I begin searching up on the third floor, while Christopher and Roderick start on the second.

All the third-floor rooms are unoccupied right now. Keith and Christopher usually block off the week of the fall lecture series for a thorough cleaning of the house and making needed repairs, so until Raphael's arrival, Anna, Taylor, and I were the only guests.

Just thinking about Taylor makes my heart pound and sets off a panic inside me, but realizing I'll be no good to her if I let that happen, I'm trying to place who she is to me and how I feel about her inside a vault deep inside me and lock it up tightly. Unless I approach this like I would any other missing child case, work it the way I would if she were a stranger—some random plumber's daughter—I might as well be a plumber.

I've got to find her. I've got to focus. I've got to let everything else go. I've got to compartmentalize. I've got to stop being her dad, at least psychologically, and just be the investigator hunting for her.

On the landing, surrounded by the five doors, Keith says, "Where do you want to start?"

I point to a door. Not because it matters which one we start with—all the rooms are the same and we have to search all of them—but because we can't afford to waste any time at all, not even seconds on indecision.

"All the rooms up here are the same," he says as he unlocks the door. "At least in terms of size and layout. Not in terms of theme and decoration."

We enter the Faye Dunaway room, which is part *Bonnie and Clyde* and part *Chinatown*, and begin to look around, though I can tell immediately that no living human beings are in this room.

We check under the bed, in the closet, in the dresser drawers, and then, as he checks the bathroom, I step over to the window and look out.

The Faye Dunaway is on the back of the house on the third floor. From it, I scan the area below.

Looking straight down, I can see the small group keeping an eye on the back door. Looking back up to the left and right I realize that from this location I can't really see into the backyards of the other houses from here.

But what I can see are the woods directly behind the house where we were searching just a few hours ago and where Vic Frankford found the Toy Story pajamas.

The night is dark and nearly moonless, cloud coverage obscuring any stars that might otherwise be visible.

I can see one of the bright beams of the flashlights Anna and the two deputies are using. The light looks lonely in the dark, dense woods—like a lone car on a canyon road. In a few moments, the other flashlights join it and the pace and movement of all three increase and together look like rural children playing hide and seek in the safe little forest beside their home in a far more innocent time.

Keith and I step back into the hall and repeat the same actions with the other rooms on the floor, which include Sidney Poitier, Zora Neale Hurston, Jim Morrison, and Butterfly McQueen, and find exactly what we did in the first one.

As we enter each new room, I'm filled with dread at what we might find. Searching a huge house room by room for my little girl makes me feel more like John Ramsey than John Jordan, and I beg God not to find what he found.

As I turn from the window in the last room on the floor, I notice Keith pulling on the mantel above the fireplace.

"What're you doing?" I ask.

"Just making sure it's locked," he says. "When do you want to check the escape room and the secret passageways?"

"This room has access to them too?" I ask. "I thought only the Zora Neal Hurston room up here did?"

He shakes his head. "That's just the one we showed you so you could see what they're like," he said. "All the rooms have fake fireplaces that are doors to the passageways behind the walls. We keep them locked. I'm just checking to make sure they all still are."

"All the rooms on the third floor or all the guest rooms?" I ask. "I thought y'all said just one on each floor did."

"All the rooms do."

"Including *ours*?" I ask, and head for our room. "So that's how whoever took Taylor got into our room."

He follows me, matching my pace.

"Maybe," he says. "But it should be locked. We're missing one of the key cards, so it could've been used. All whoever has it would have to do is reprogram it with the machine on the desk in the parlor when no one was looking."

"*Should* be locked?" I ask. "I didn't even know our room had one."

"Sorry if we weren't clear about that," he says. "I thought you knew."

"We wouldn't be staying in there if I had known," I say. "I'd never knowingly expose Taylor to that kind of risk."

"I feel terrible," he said. "I'm so sorry I wasn't clear when we took you through it."

My focus and energy is directed toward getting to our room and checking the fireplace, but as he says that I wonder if he really is sorry or if the omission was intentional.

31

When we reach the second-floor landing, Roderick and Christopher are coming out of the room between ours and Hal Raphael's.

"Anything?" Roderick asks.

I shake my head. "No. Y'all?"

"Nothing."

"Have y'all checked our room again yet?" I ask.

"Was just about to."

I place my key card into the reader on the door handle.

Keith says to Christopher, "You been checking the fireplaces?"

When my key card won't read, I glance back at the others and then try again.

Christopher, who seems out of it, says, "No. Why?"

"I have," Roderick says. "They've all been clear."

"I meant to make sure they're locked," Keith says.

"Locked?" Roderick asks.

"They're the doors to the secret passageway that runs from the escape room to the back of the house."

"*All* of them?" Roderick asks. "I thought—"

"Yeah," Keith says. "Only two are direct exits from the escape room, but they all access the passageway. The only working fireplace in the house is in the parlor. But they all lock from the inside of the room like connecting doors in hotel rooms."

"For some reason my key won't work," I say, then to Keith. "Will you try yours?"

"That's strange. Sure."

He steps up and tries his master key card and it works the first time.

I rush into the room to find it just as we had left it. I run over to the fireplace and turn toward Keith. "How does it work?" I ask. "Will you see if it's locked?"

He steps over and runs his fingers along the underside of the right end of the wooden mantel. Finding the button, he presses it. Following the pop of a latch from inside, the left side of the fireplace slowly swivels open a few inches with a low creak.

He shakes his head. "It wasn't locked."

"We need to search the passageways and the escape room," I say.

"We'll start from the escape room and come this way," Roderick says.

"I can't do this again," Christopher is saying.

"You don't have to," Keith says. "Let Roderick into the escape room, show him an exit to access the passageways, and then go lie down on the couch in the parlor. I'll be in to check on you as soon as I can."

Christopher mumbles something but I am too far into the passageway to make it out.

Tapping on the flashlight on my phone, I scan the narrow, all-black passageway—first in one direction and then the other.

The light from my phone doesn't have much reach and I wonder what's in the darkness beyond its illumination.

In another moment Keith joins me, the light of his phone joining mine.

"Are there any lights in here?" I ask.

"No, sorry," he says. "We could really use some strong flashlights. Want me to go get—"

"I don't want to wait another second to search back here."

"I understand," he says. "Let's do it."

"You lead the way," I say. "Take us through the best, quickest way possible, but make sure we cover every inch."

"Will do."

32

"We should check each second-floor room's entry into the passageway while we're here," he says. "Each one is set back a little and feeds into this main hallway at different points, which is probably why you didn't notice them when we were in here before. Well, that and the fact that it's coal mine black in here. We also need to check the entryway and small room directly off of the landing."

We do as he says and check each of the entryways from the second-floor rooms and the landing. The quick search into each yields nothing.

"Okay," he says, "we'll go down the main hallway now."

I follow him down the dark, narrow hallway that reminds me of a walk-through amusement park haunted house, unable to see anything but the back of his shirt—and that only in flashes as my phone moves up and down with the movements of my hands.

We bounce around, careening off one wall only to slam into the other—like mice in a too-small black box maze.

The floor we are running on is just plywood subfloor that has been painted black. It gives and creaks and groans as we move over it, each of our footfalls sounding as if we are stomping as violently as we can. We're making a lot of noise, but if someone wanted to pass through these passageways quietly it would certainly be possible.

Eventually we reach the stairs in the back that lead down to the residence and up to the third floor. When he stops at them I run into him.

"Sorry," he says. "Should've warned you we were stopping."

I hold my light up and out to the side so I can see his face without shining the light directly into his eyes.

"It's okay," I say. "I'm the one who told you to go as fast as you could."

"We have three options," he says. "We can go downstairs to the residence, upstairs to the third floor, or circle back to the escape room."

"Roderick will be coming from the escape room and should see everything between it and wherever we encounter him, so let's go up and check the third floor first, then come back down and check the stairs down to the residence, then we can go toward the escape room."

"Sounds good," he says, and turns and starts up the stairs.

I follow—though not quite as closely this time, partly to keep from running into him, but mostly because the small, narrow stairway makes it impossible.

We check the third-floor passageway and all the rooms' entryways into it, as well as the small room and entryway off the landing, exactly what we did on the second floor.

We then move back down the way we came—down the dark hallway, down the stairs, this time taking the stairs all the way to the first floor before heading back toward the escape room.

About halfway to the escape room we meet up with Roderick. "Anything?" he asks.

"No," I say. "You?"

"Nothing," he says. "Where the hell can she be? No one has left the house and we've searched everything, right?"

"The only thing left is the residence," I say. "And with the cameras disconnected, we don't know that someone didn't leave the house with her before we even knew she was gone."

"Yeah, I guess I meant since we've been aware of her being missing."

"How is Chris?" Keith asks him.

"Not great," he said. "He's lying down on one of the couches in the parlor."

"Y'all mind if we go to the residence that way, so we can get him and take him with us? I'm worried about him."

"That's fine," I say. "Lead the way."

He does.

33

"If whoever abducted Taylor was in the passageway behind the fireplace and entered our room shortly after the last time I checked on her," I say, "then he or she had about a fifteen- or twenty-minute head start."

We are back on the first floor in the main part of the house. Keith and Christopher are leading Roderick and me back to their residence.

"Which was plenty of time to get her out of the house," I continue. "But since we could all see the front door, they had to use the back door."

With everyone but the four of us outside searching for Taylor or watching the doors, the house seems even bigger and simultaneously quieter and creakier.

"The fact that everyone from the night Magdalene was abducted was in the parlor and dining room with you when it happened bolsters the theory that it was someone from outside of the house who broke in," Roderick says.

"Not everyone from that night was with us," I say. "Hal Raphael wasn't. Neither was Rake Sabin for much of the time, who was supposed to be up there watching him."

"Oh, that's right."

"And neither was Henrique Arango," I say, "but he was with us in the parlor the entire time he was here and we saw him leave through the front door and we have a witness—Derinda Dacosta—who followed him out."

"Plus he's a sick old man," he says. "I know we can't be 100 percent certain, but I think we got the roadblocks up before whoever has her would've been able to leave town with her."

"That's why a thorough search, beginning in the house and moving outward is so critical," I say.

Keith unlocks the door leading to their residence and we walk down the short hallway, around a laundry basket of folded sheets, a cleaning cart, and a couple of boxes of Halloween decorations.

When we arrive in the residence kitchen, Christopher, who still hasn't uttered a word, collapses into one of the chairs at the table.

Keith says, "Do you want me to lead you through or do you want us to sit here while you look around?"

"If you don't mind," I say, "probably go quicker with you taking us through."

He shakes his head. "Of course not. Don't mind at all. Want to do anything I can to help you find your daughter." He looks down at Christopher. "You okay to sit here for a minute while I show them around?"

He nods. "I'm fine. I'm just done. This just brings it all up again and I'm completely spent. Having nothing left."

"Just sit here and rest. We'll be back in a minute. You want some water or anything?"

"Just go. I'm okay."

"Okay. I'll be back in just a few. Let me dim the lights in here for you. Lay your head down on the table and rest."

Keith turns on the small light under the oven hood and then turns off the harsh overhead light.

"We can start with this supply closet," he says, indicating the first door of the hallway leading back toward the bed and breakfast part of the house.

He steps over and opens the door and turns on the light inside.

"We mostly keep the B&B supplies in here, but there are a few of our own also."

Roderick and I step over and look inside.

It's a ten by ten closet with floor-to-ceiling shelves filled with cleaning supplies, boxes of small hotel toiletries, pillows, blankets, sheets, wall art, and various other random guest services supplies.

There is nowhere inside big enough for Taylor to be hidden.

As we step back, Keith quickly grabs the boxes, laundry basket, and cleaning cart from the hallway and puts them inside the closet before closing the door.

"What is that flickering?" Christopher says.

We turn to see him sitting up and looking down the other end of the hallway at Magdalene's bedroom door.

"It's . . ." He jumps up. "Look. See that. Flickering lights and shadows. Someone is in Magdalene's room."

We follow his gaze to the light and movement coming from beneath the closed door of Magdalene's room.

He's right. It appears as if someone is inside her room.

I glance at Keith. "Did y'all leave any lights on in there?"

His eyes are as wide as Christopher's, his expression just as anxious and perplexed.

"No," he says. "Never. There's no light like that in there anyway. That looks like— Is it a fire?"

Roderick and I both withdraw our weapons and, holding them down at our sides, move over to the door.

He puts his hand on the knob and looks at me.

I nod.

He turns the knob and pushes open the door.

And we stare in shock and horror at the body of the little girl on the bed.

34

The light and movement we had seen beneath the door is from flickering candles surrounding the bed and the body on it.

Heat from the half-burned candles wafts out of the room through the door, over us, and into the kitchen.

There's a disconnect between what I'm seeing and any thoughts my mind can form from it, a visual cognitive dissonance that is surreal and unsettling.

In the glow of the candlelight the room looks like a sanctuary, the bed an altar, the little girl in the white gown on it perhaps part of a pagan rite or funereal ritual.

The body of the beautiful little girl laid out on the bed is clearly lifeless, unmoving, inanimate, the castoff remnants of a mortal coil.

Flashes of Taylor streak the night sky of my mind like heat lightning on a hot summer night.

But the body on the bed is not Taylor, but the little girl who the bed belongs to.

Magdalene, as if frozen in time somehow, is back in her bed looking much as she did the night she vanished, only instead of sweet, cutesy Toy Story pajamas, she's sheathed in an elegant white gown.

Suddenly, jarringly, I become aware of Keith and Christopher screaming and yelling and trying to press past us as and Roderick and I block the doorway into the room that is a crime scene for a second time.

"Oh, God," Christopher screams. "Oh, God."

Roderick holsters his weapon, snatches the radio off his belt and calls for backup.

"Let us in to check on her," Keith is saying.

"I'm sorry," I say. "We can't."

"She's gone, Keith," Roderick says. "It's obvious. I'm sorry. We've got to preserve the scene now so we can find out who did this to her."

"She's just sleeping," Christopher says.

"You've got to let us check," Keith says.

"Keith," I say, my voice calm but firm, "she wouldn't still look like she did nearly a year ago."

"How . . ." he says, looking up at her again. "How . . . is that . . . possible?"

"We're gonna find out," Roderick says.

"Who would do this?" Keith says. "Who could do something like this? Wasn't enough to take her from us, they have to . . . to . . . to bring her back to . . . to torture and taunt us like this."

"Oh God," Christopher keeps saying between sobs and screams and yells. "Oh, God."

A deputy opens the hallway door and asks Roderick how he can help.

Before Roderick can respond, Derinda, who is behind the deputy with a few other people, sees how upset Keith and Christopher are.

"WHAT IS IT?" she yells. "WHAT'S WRONG?"

"It's her, Mama," Keith says. "It's our little Magdalene."

"What?" she says. "What do you mean? It's her what?"

Derinda rushes past the deputy over to Keith, who is nearest the hallway.

"*What* is it?" she asks.

But before he can respond, she turns and looks through the open door into the room where we're all looking and begins to scream. If possible her cries seem even more inconsolable than Keith's and Christopher's, and I wonder if it's because she's grieving for both her child and her grandchild.

"Help them into the front room," Roderick says to the deputy, "and stay with them. No one else comes in here. Tell everyone to keep looking for Taylor. Everybody keep doing what they're doing. I'm calling FDLE and the medical examiner's office. Bring them right back to us when they get here."

35

"Have you ever seen anything like this?" Roderick is asking. "I'm not just talking about the way the body is displayed like this with all the candles and everything. I mean finding her dead back in her bed nearly a year after she was taken."

I shake my head.

We're next to the bed, looking down at Magdalene's little body.

The medical examiner and FDLE are on the way.

We have already taken pictures and video of every inch of the room and the body and have just finished extinguishing the candles.

Magdalene looks as if she hasn't aged a day, as if we've come in here on December 23 of last year and found her like this. Not only this, but there are no signs of violence, no obvious cause of death. It's as if she's merely sleeping peacefully in her own bed.

It's obvious her body has been recently bathed and her hair washed, and the gown she has on is spotless, pristine.

"But . . ." Roderick is saying, "for her to look like this—like she did when she was abducted—she'd have to have been killed back then, ten months ago. How is that possible? How can she look so . . . She looks like she just died. Of course, maybe she did. But if she did, how did she not age in the past year?"

"I'm sure the autopsy will tell us," I say. "But either way I'm pretty sure it needs to be performed as quickly as possible."

"Medical examiner should be here in a few."

"Good."

"But why?" he asks.

"If I had to guess, I'd say she was killed shortly after the time she was taken."

Even as I say it I try not to think about whether Taylor has already suffered the same fate.

My first priority is finding Taylor, but with so many people out looking for her and the roadblocks in place, I've made the calculation that the best way to do that is to keep investigating Magdalene's disappearance and death. It could be the total wrong choice. I have no way of knowing. I'm trying to block everything out and just concentrate on the crime scene before me, but I'm finding it extremely difficult.

"The most likely reason is that she's been frozen since then," I continue. "I've read about cases and seen crime scene and autopsy photographs where the victim had been frozen. That would explain why she appears not to have aged. I could be wrong about any of this. It has been a while since I've read about it. But if that's what has happened, her body will thaw from the outside in, so there might still be frozen areas and ice crystals inside. Since cells are mostly water, when they freeze ice crystals are formed and fracture the cells in a recognizable pattern. Depending on how long her body has been thawing . . . how much of the tissue is still intact and not decayed, the ME should be able to tell if her body has been frozen. And hopefully be able to determine cause of death, but the longer it takes to perform the autopsy the less likely any of that becomes. Especially toxicology."

He nods and lets out a little whistle. "Wow. If you're right . . . then she's been kept in a freezer somewhere for nearly a year."

I nod.

"So we need to look at freezers," he says. "Who has a freezer big enough to hold a body and not be seen for almost a year?"

I frown and my eyes sting. "Small body," I say. "It wouldn't require a very big freezer, but restaurants have large walk-in freezers that a body could easily be hidden in."

"The Samuelsons?" he asks.

"I'm not saying it's them. I'm just trying to answer your question. A lot of these places around here are rentals. Nobody thinks twice about a lock on a cabinet or a closet or a freezer."

"That's true. But no matter where the body was stored . . . why take the risk of . . . putting her back in her bed? And why now?"

"The answers to those two questions could very well be the keys to close the case," I say.

"Any ideas?"

I shake my head. "Not really. But you're right about it being an enormous risk. Must be a good reason."

"Wouldn't be a risk if she was—if her body was already in the house," he says. "Did it strike you as suspicious that they led us right to her? Christopher can't help us look anymore . . . so he supposedly sits in the parlor. But that means he was the only one not being watched at the time. He could've come back here and lit the candles during that time. Why did they wait to bring us back here until last thing? Why didn't they tell either one of us about all the rooms having access to the secret passageway? Think about it . . . he sat down on the side of the table where he was looking in the right direction to see her room. We're in here less than five minutes and he's yelling he sees light and movement in the room."

I nod. "I agree. It's all suspicious. No one else could have taken her out of her room originally or put her back into her room tonight more easily than the two of them. And you're right about the other things being suspicious. The only thing I'd say is that I don't think the candles were lit during the time Christopher wasn't with us. Doesn't mean he or they didn't light them, but they had been burning a while. Most of the candles were burned about halfway down, and I'd say they could have been lit before and just relit recently, but the heat that came out of the room makes me think they were lit a lot longer this time."

He purses his lips and thinks about it. "You're probably right. But like you say, that doesn't mean they didn't do it earlier."

DAY 191

Day 191

I've never had a hard time sleeping. But since Magdalene was taken I can't sleep, and if I do it's only for moments at a time and I wake up panicked from nightmares. Keith has always had a hard time sleeping and Magdalene struggled some too, but I never have until now. I can't imagine I'll ever sleep well again. Keith keeps trying to get me to take something but I don't know. I've seen some of the things he's done in his sleep while on the medication and it scares me. I don't wanna be that out of control, but I've got to get some sleep or I'm going to shoot myself in the head.

36

W hile the medical examiner—who came herself and didn't just send the investigator on call—examines the body and Roderick calls his sheriff to let him know what's going on, I choose a picture of Taylor and write the details for the Amber Alert, and then search the rest of the residence.

Wishing Anna was here to help me, I wonder how her search is going and begin missing her terribly—missing far more the person she had been up until a few weeks ago than anything else.

There aren't many rooms—a small den, Magdalene's bathroom, an office/workout room, a laundry room, and Keith and Christopher's master suite.

Everything everywhere is neat and tidy, clean, immaculate.

Many of the furnishings appear to be authentic antiques, but I wouldn't know if they weren't—unless it was painfully obvious.

There is no sign of Taylor—or that she was here at any point tonight—and I don't find any additional hidden rooms or secret passageways.

But I do find a few things I have questions about—and a couple of them are both suspicious and alarming.

In the laundry room, which is on the west side of the house, I find a Frigidaire 8.7-cubic-foot manual-defrost chest freezer, which itself is suspicious given the circumstances of Magdalene's reappearance, but the fact that it is empty, its removable basket missing, and it has recently been cleaned with bleach, is unnerving.

I make a note to get FDLE to process it.

Curious, if not suspicious, is the fact that there are both cat and dog bowls, a couple of kennels, and even a PetSafe wall-entry pet door of about 12 by 18 inches, and yet I have seen no evidence of or heard anyone mention pets of any kind while we've been here this week.

But by far the most red-flag-raising item I encounter is the sheer number of sleep aid medications. There are no less than four over-the-counter sleep aids—two for adults, two for children and sensitive adults—between Keith and Christopher's bathroom and Magdalene's. It's excessive by any standard, but given that mixed in with it are bottles of Benadryl, melatonin, and prescription sleeping pills, it is staggering.

After making notes about and taking pictures of these items of interest, I walk back toward Magdalene's bedroom.

Her body has been removed and is on its way to the morgue. Roderick and the ME are standing outside Magdalene's door talking.

"John Jordan, this is Dr. Jennifer Gottschall."

She's a tall, thin woman in her late forties with black hair and blue eyes.

"I'm so sorry to hear about your daughter," she says.

"Thank you."

"Rod told me what you said about the body having been frozen," she says. "I think you're right. I'm actually going to perform the autopsy tonight—as soon as I get back. We're going to rush everything—all the labs and toxicology—and see if what we find can help you find your daughter."

"Thank you very much," I say. "I sure appreciate that."

Roderick's radio sounds and the deputy on the front door tells them there are people here to see me.

He looks at me.

I shrug.

"We're on our way," he says into the radio, then to Dr. Gottschall, "We'll walk you out."

A few minutes later, I step through the front door to see Merrill, Dad, Jake, Verna, and Reggie, and tears sting my eyes.

After quick hugs, Merrill says, "We're here to help. Tell us what we can do."

"Roderick Brandt, this is my dad Jack Jordan and his wife Verna, my brother Jake, my best friend Merrill Monroe, and the sheriff of Gulf County, Reggie Summers. They've got a lot of experience and training."

"Nice to meet y'all," Roderick says. "And we appreciate your willingness to help. We can use it."

He begins to assign them various tasks and searching details but before he finishes, his radio sounds again.

It's one of the deputies searching the woods behind the house with Anna.

At first we can't understand what he's saying.

"Repeat that please," Roderick says.

"It's Mrs. Jordan. She collapsed and is unconscious."

DAY 205

Day 205

Is it possible that we poisoned our own daughter? Did I give her any sleeping medication that night? I honestly can't remember. Maybe I did and maybe I forgot and then maybe Keith did and maybe we killed a little girl without even realizing it.

37

By the time we get to the backyard, the two deputies are emerging from the woods carrying Anna.

I rush over to her.

She's breathing fine, but is not conscious.

"ETA on the ambulance is six minutes," Roderick says.

"What do you want us to do with her?" the younger deputy asks.

"We can't take her inside," Roderick says. "It's a crime scene and it's swarming with FDLE techs."

I pull off my shirt and lay it on the ground.

"Just lay her here for a moment," I say.

They start to ease her down, but Merrill has them wait while he takes his shirt off and lays it down too. A few others around us follow suit—including Clarence Samuelson, Rake Sabin, and Scott Haskew.

With the makeshift shirt pallet in place, the two deputies lay Anna down.

Kneeling beside her, I touch her face and say her name.

"We were just walking along searching one minute and she was on the ground the next," the older deputy says. "Seems fine otherwise—like maybe she just fainted or something. I'm sure she's exhausted and overwrought."

"She's probably dehydrated too," Rake says.

"Anna," I say again, louder this time, and shake her a little. "Anna, can you hear me?"

She stirs a little, mumbling something and attempting to open her eyes.

"Anna?"

She tries to open her eyes a few times, but it takes several tries for her to keep them open.

"Hey," I say.

"What is . . . John? What's . . . What are you doing?"

"How do you feel?" I ask.

"What happened?"

"You passed out," I say. "You were in the woods."

"Oh, no," she says. "Taylor. Someone has Taylor. We've got to find her."

She tries to get up. She doesn't get very far.

"We will," I say. "But right now we've got to get you to the hospital."

"No," she says. "No way I'm leaving. I've got to find my baby and get her back."

"A lot of people are looking," I say. "We're gonna find her. They'll keep looking while we get you checked out."

"I'm not going to the goddamn hospital," she says. "Not while my little Taylor is out there somewhere with God knows what happening to her. Absolutely no way."

Rake brings a bottle of water for her and hands it to me.

"Drink some of this," I say.

I cup my hand behind her head and tilt it up slightly with one hand while holding the open bottle to her lips with the other.

She drinks a few sips and tries to get up again, but again is unable.

"You've got to let them check you out," I say.

She tries to get up again. It goes about as well as the other times.

"Let them see what's wrong with you and you'll be back out here in no time, okay?"

"I'm not stayin'," she says. "No matter what they say."

"You don't have to," I say. "Let's just get you checked out and then we'll be right back out here. Okay?"

"I won't stay no matter what they say," she repeats. "And I won't go unless you stay here and keep working on finding her. That's the only way I'll go."

"I want to be with you," I say.

"What matters more to me?" she says. "Having you with me or knowing you're out here trying to find Taylor?"

"You can't go alone," I say.

"We need everyone out here looking for—"

"I'll go with you," Verna says, stepping over to where Anna can see her. "I'll go. I'll take good care of her and y'all can keep looking for Taylor."

Anna nods.

"Quit wasting time with me," Anna says to me. "Go find Taylor."

I notice that she hasn't once referred to Taylor as *our* little girl, only as hers—as *her little Taylor*—or simply as Taylor.

"Go," she says. "Now. Go find her."

I lean down and kiss Anna and tell her I love her.

She doesn't respond—to the kiss or the words.

"Merrill and I will carry you to the ambulance," I say, "then we'll get back to work on finding Taylor."

"Merrill's here?" she says. "Merrill. Find my baby for me, Merrill. I know you can."

"We will," he says. "You just relax and work on gettin' better. We'll find her."

DAY 210

Day 210

Where is my baby girl right now? What is she doing? Is she okay? Is someone caring for her, doting on her? Is someone using and abusing her? Is her cold body decaying in the cold ground somewhere?

I miss you so much I can't breathe.

Please come home to us. Please. Please. Please. Please. Please.

38

W hile Verna accompanies Anna to the hospital and
Roderick gives everyone their assignments, I step
inside to speak with Keith and Christopher.

They are in the parlor with Derinda, who is comforting
them.

Keith is half propped on the left arm of the couch, one foot
on the floor. Christopher is sitting on that end, next to and
below Keith. Derinda is next to Christopher.

They are sniffling as tears trickle down their cheeks, and
not only are they sitting as closely as they can to each other but
they are continually touching and patting each other in
comfort and consolation.

I'm surprised the FDLE crime scene unit has allowed them
to remain in the house, but they have—with the understanding
that they will confine themselves to the parlor and dining
room.

"I guess some part of me was holding out hope that she
could still be alive and we'd get her back somehow," Christopher says. "It's so much more real now—in a way it never was

before. And for your little Taylor to be taken too. It's . . . just . . . too, too . . ."

"I just wanted to say again how sorry I am that this has happened," Keith says. "For it to happen once in our home is . . . But twice . . . I just feel so bad."

Derinda says, "It just doesn't seem real. I just can't . . . It's like my mind can't accept that . . . "

"And to find Magdalene . . ." Christopher says. "Our sweet little Magdalene . . . dead . . . and displayed like that. Who would . . ."

"I'm gonna do my best to find out who did that to Magdalene, who has Taylor," I say. "What they've done, they've done to both of our families. And I need to ask you a few more questions to clear a few things up."

Keith nods. "Of course," he says. "Anything."

"During our search of the house for Taylor . . . we noticed quite a lot of sleeping medication—both prescription and over the counter and for adults and children."

"I've always had a hard time sleeping," Keith says. "I used to take sleep aids all the time. Didn't help much, but enough to keep me trying. I don't take them like I used to. I bet if you look at the expiration dates of most of them they'll be expired. We need to throw them out, but . . . there's a lot we need to do that we haven't gotten to yet."

"He doesn't use it like he used to," Christopher repeats. "Made him do some strange and dangerous things in his sleep."

"After what happened to Magdalene," Keith says, "I just gave up on sleeping."

"Ironically, that's when so many friends and family brought us the stuff," Christopher says. "That's why there's so much of it —and why most of it isn't opened."

"Some of it is for adults and some for children," I say. "Did Magdalene ever take it?"

I ask *did Magdalene ever take it* instead of *did you ever give it to her* to try to sound less accusatory.

"Not often, no," Keith says. "Maybe a few times during the entire time we had her. And that was mostly at the very beginning when she was getting adjusted. You'll notice the packages say 'for children and sensitive adults.' Those were mostly for Christopher. He's very sensitive to medication."

"Did Magdalene take any the night of the solstice party when she went missing?"

Christopher shrugs and says, "I don't think so."

"No," Keith says. "She absolutely did not." He looks at Christopher. "She definitely didn't. How can you shrug and say you don't think so?"

"I'm just not sure anymore," he says.

"Well, I am."

"Okay," Christopher says, as if trying to placate a bully.

"Sorry," Keith says, "but one of the crazy conspiracy theories out there is that we overdosed her on sleeping pills and this whole thing is just some elaborate cover-up. It just . . . it's gets me going. Sorry."

I decide to leave this for now, but plan to come back to it at some point.

"I noticed you have a lot of pet paraphernalia," I say, "but I haven't seen any pets since we've been here."

"We tried both a dog and a cat for Magdalene," Keith says, "but neither worked out."

"The poor dear was allergic," Derinda says.

"She wasn't the only one," Christopher says. "Between the two of us I bet we went through a gallon of Benadryl while we had the damned things."

"See," Keith says, "when you say things like that some people might take you literally and then it gives credence to the theory that we somehow overdosed our daughter."

"I just meant—I wasn't being literal."

Keith looks at me. "But we also have all the supplies because some of our guests bring pets. They're not allowed in the rooms, so we offer a sort of kennel service for them—take care of them overnight while their owners are staying with us."

"Did Magdalene still have a pet on the night she was abducted?"

"I still can't believe she's dead," Christopher says, more tears streaming down his cheeks. "And left like that in her bed for us to find."

Keith and Derinda both pat him and wipe at tears of their own.

Keith says, "She still had the cat. Sammy Socks. We finally got rid of him shortly after . . . after . . . that night. Henrique took him."

"Which made no sense," Christopher says. "He left right after that for three months. He had to know he was about to leave when he took him from us."

I start to ask them about the freezer, but decide to wait to see what FDLE finds out about it first. Instead I broach a subject that I had wanted to talk to Keith and Christopher about individually, but now don't feel like I have the time to wait to get them alone.

"I've got one more question for you guys," I say, "and it may be sensitive, but my goal is only to find Magdalene's killer and get my daughter back. The clock is ticking, which means I have to be more blunt than I usually am, use less finesse."

Keith sits up a little straighter and seems to set himself in a defensive posture, as Christopher's eyebrows raise up.

"In Christopher's journal . . ." I say.

"I knew this was going to happen," Keith says. "I told him he was insane for including his journal in the casebook. They're just his ramblings, his random, vulnerable thoughts."

"Go ahead," Christopher says to me. "I stand by everything I wrote."

"You talk about guilt you feel about what y'all did that night," I say. "You speak about being so angry at Keith you weren't sure you could ever forgive him or be intimate with him again."

"For fuck sake," Keith says. "You put that in your journal?"

"I need to know why that is," I say. "What that's about. What happened that night that made you feel that way? What do you feel so guilty about? Because several of the others who were there that night noticed you guys disappeared for a while during the party."

Christopher looks up at Keith.

Keith shakes his head and says, "We really gonna do this?"

"We have to."

"Unbelievable," he says, still shaking his head and looking disgusted, then to his mother, "Could you excuse us for a few minutes?"

"No," Christopher says. "No one has been more supportive of us than Derinda. I feel almost like she's as much my mother as yours. I want her to stay. She should know too."

"Still looking for ways to punish me, aren't you?" Keith says. "Okay. Fine. Take your best shot. Humiliate and embarrass me in front of my own mother. I don't care anymore."

"Let me start by saying I have forgiven Keith," Christopher says. "Despite what he might think. And I'm not doing this to embarrass or punish anyone. I just want absolutely everything out in the open."

He reaches up and takes Keith's hand.

"At a certain point in our relationship," Christopher says, "the point where everything else was as good as it could be—our family, our child, our business, our relationships with friends and family, which is probably not a coincidence—Keith decided he was a little bored with our sex life."

"Not bored," Keith says. "That's unfair."

"A little restless," Christopher says. "Anyway. He decided he wanted to shake things up a little bit. And this was about the time—probably also not a coincidence—that Scott Haskew expressed interest in having a threesome with us."

Keith is looking down now, avoiding eye contact with anyone, especially his mother.

"So after a while of talking and planning and negotiating and preparing . . ." Christopher says, "we decided that the three of us would sneak into the escape room during the party for a quick little ménage à trois. That's it. That's what we did—that's where we were when our friends said we disappeared. And I wasn't mad at Keith for wanting to try it. I was mad at him and I feel guilty about the fact that while our little girl was being kidnapped and murdered, instead of protecting her we were in the escape room with our dicks out acting like much younger men with much less responsibility."

Keith begins to cry. "I'm so sorry," he says. "If my . . . If I'm the reason she was killed."

His mom hops up from the couch and goes around to him and hugs him.

"You are most certainly *not* the reason she was—that what happened to her happened. Neither of you are."

"We'd never done anything like that before," Keith says.

"Oh, my sweet boy," she says. "You didn't do anything wrong. Y'all are not the reason she was taken. What you were doing didn't cause her to get taken. Do you think if you had been in the parlor with the rest of them instead of the escape room that she wouldn't have been taken?"

"She's right," I say. "What happened to Magdalene isn't your fault and it isn't because of what you were doing. And if you don't believe me, just think about this . . . Anna and I weren't in the escape room. Anna was in the bed with Taylor and I was in the parlor where you would've been if you hadn't gone into the escape room that night, and Taylor was still taken."

That seems to make an impact. A slight change in posture

and their breathing seems to convey a certain lifting of the burden of guilt they had been carrying since that night.

All three of them are crying now, but the tears seem more like tears of release, of loss and sorrow instead of guilt and recrimination.

For a few moments no one says anything. I wait as the three of them cry and comfort and console one another, thinking about Anna, Taylor, and Johanna and longing for us all to be together as I do.

Eventually, Derinda says, "Can we ask *you* a question?"

"Of course."

"Who could do such a thing?" she asks. "What kind of criminal could take a precious little girl like Magdalene, kill her, then put her back in her bed like that for the boys to find? What kind of sick psychopath does something so cruel and unusual and dramatic like that?"

"A very specific one," I say. "With some unique fantasies and proclivities that will actually help us catch him. And that's exactly what I intend to do."

DAY 214

Day 214

   The books that Wren is bringing us are becoming more and more bizarre. What am I missing? How do all the crazy conspiracy theories making the rounds these days have anything to do with me wanting to die because someone took my daughter? Is she really saying I should check the nearest pizza place so see if Magdalene is part of some child sex ring operating out of the back office? WTF?

39

"FDLE is done here," Roderick is saying. "They're rushing everything—have actually called staff back into the lab tonight who will be waiting for the evidence when the crime scene unit gets back with it."

I nod. "That's great. I really appreciate that."

We are standing in the hallway separating the B&B from the residence and have the door closed for privacy, even though as far as we know the only other people in the house are Keith, Christopher, and Derinda, and they are in the parlor.

"ME is already performing the autopsy," he says, "so we should have the prelim autopsy results and the lab work by early in the morning. Also said depending on what they test for —and assuming there's enough viable tissue to test—certain toxicology tests, like a general drug screen, can be done in a matter of hours. So if she was drugged and it wasn't with something too exotic, we should know about that tomorrow too."

"Gives us our greatest chance of finding Taylor quickly and alive."

"They left it up to me as to whether to let people back in the house or not," he says. "I was thinking about just sealing off

Magdalene's room and your room and letting everybody back in. We really need it as a staging area for our search and I'd like to keep as close an eye on everyone as possible. I like the idea of having them here with us and interacting with each other. What do you think?"

I nod. "I agree. That's a great idea."

"We're gonna find her," he says. "Promise you that. Won't stop until we do."

I get the worst sense of fear and foreboding when he says that, and I wish he hadn't, but I don't say anything, just nod.

An awkward moment passes between us.

He looks away, back toward the residence. "They took the entire freezer with them," he says. "I cleared the backyard and had them take it out that way so no one would see. Obviously if we let Keith and Christopher back in here they will notice it's gone, but . . . we can just deal with that when they ask."

I nod again. "Speaking of freezers," I say, "we should use the search for Taylor to look in as many as we can—including the commercial ones in town, like at The Sand Witch."

"Will do. What else?"

"I'm sure you've thought of this . . ." I say. "I'm not saying it because I don't think you have, but we need to search carefully every empty house, rental, and place under construction. If the roadblock turned them around, then he may have her in one of those type places trying to outwait us."

He nods enthusiastically. "One of the teams has a rental agent with a master key with them."

"Perfect."

"I've been trying to track everyone's movements tonight," he says. "When your wife began screaming, everyone was together in the parlor and dining room except for Hal Raphael. You can actually attest to that. You were in there too. And they were in there a good while even before you got there. Correct me if I'm wrong about any of this: You checked on Taylor and she was fine. You spoke briefly to Rake and Charis on the landing, then you and Charis came down and joined the others. Eventually Rake comes down for some food, and though he intends to go right back up he never does. Then Haskins and I come in and talk for a few minutes. And your wife starts screaming that Taylor's gone. Is that right?"

I nod.

"That's a narrow window," he says. "Very narrow. So, like the night Magdalene was taken, either someone broke in or someone inside took her—and the only two people who were here on the night of Magdalene's disappearance and who weren't accounted for while Taylor was being taken are Rake Sabin and Hal Raphael—assuming Taylor was taken before Rake came downstairs, which seems likely. And when I was wondering which one it could be, I started thinking . . . What if they're in it together? What if Rake's accusations and the bad things he has to say about Raphael are a cover? After all it was Rake who volunteered to go up there and keep an eye on Raphael. No one asked him to. What if that, like all his negative comments, was just a ruse?"

DAY 219

Day 219

Demi Gonzalez, our adoption agent, told us that given what happened to Magdalene, the chances of us being able to adopt again are very slim.

The strangest, most disturbing thing about that is not that it means she or they or everyone blames us for what happened—as if we did or did not do something we should have to keep her safe—which I guess is what everyone thinks. (Including me sometimes, though I don't know what the hell else we could've done). No, the strangest thing is that we didn't ask. She told us this as if we had inquired about the possibility of adopting again, but we did no such thing. We have no interest in adopting again. There is no replacement for Magdalene. It would feel like such a betrayal to our little girl to say, Oh well, we lost that one, let's just get another.

40

With no need to watch the front and back doors as a group, those who had been have now joined the search, and I try to talk to them as they come in occasionally for water or to use the restroom.

To my surprise Demi Gonzalez has come back out in the middle of the night to help.

"I really appreciate you helping with the search," I say as she steps out of the bathroom and into the hallway.

"Least I could do when I heard," she says. "I'm so sorry this has happened. I just can't wrap my head around it happening twice in the same house. And, my God, poor Keith and Christopher. After all this time and to find precious little Magdalene dead in her own bed."

Her expression of sadness for Keith and Christopher reminds me to check on Charis, who is probably equally as devastated and not receiving a fraction of the support and condolences.

She starts to make her way back down the hallway, but stops and turns toward me again.

"I'm hesitant to say anything," she says. "For a variety of

reasons—including legal issues of privacy—but . . . given the circumstances . . . I know how important it is that we find your little girl as quickly as possible. This may be nothing. Probably is, but . . . I just . . . Oh, God, I feel so guilty even saying it, but . . . I feel I must. Like I say, it's probably nothing. Anyway, Brooke Wakefield has been obsessed with having a child for as long as I've known her. She's . . . She was seriously considering adoption. When I say *serious* . . . she had already converted a spare bedroom in her house into a nursery. Anyway, she kept pestering me to find her a little girl. I mean . . . she was relentless. But then after Magdalene went missing she stopped. I'm talking full stop. She went from bugging me every day about finding her a little girl to saying she has changed her mind. It was the most stark contrast I've ever seen—and I've been doing this a long time. Then a few weeks later—a few weeks after Magdalene disappeared—she started up again, bugging the fuck out of me to find her a little girl. Something she's done from then until now. But I just saw her out there while we were searching and she told me she had changed her mind again, that she no longer needed me to find her a little girl to adopt, that she was good. It probably doesn't mean anything but just in case it did I didn't want to not have told you. But given that it could cost me my job, please keep it between us."

"I will," I say. "And I really appreciate you telling me. Truly."

As soon as she walks away, I text Roderick.

Has anyone searched Brooke Wakefield's place yet?

Let me check.

A few moments later, he texts again.

No. It hasn't been done yet. I'm assuming you have a reason for asking. Want to join me for it and a search of The Sand Witch's freezers?

Yes.

Pick you up out front in five.

.   .   .

WHILE WAITING for Roderick on the narrow street at the edge of Keith and Christopher's property, various weary searchers— both civilian and law enforcement—pass by, some heading to different search locations, others heading into the Florida House for water and the restroom.

I thank each of them for what they're doing to help find Taylor and I am so grateful for the opportunity to do so.

As Roderick pulls up, I see Charis in the distance heading this way.

"Give me just a minute," I say.

I walk over to meet Charis.

"I was hoping to see you," I say. "To check on you and tell you how sorry I am about Magdalene. Sorry I haven't been able to until now."

Her eyes are red and puffy, and it's obvious she's been crying.

"That's so thoughtful of you," she says, "but don't you dare apologize for anything. With what you're dealing with right now . . . It means all the more that you thought of me."

"And thank you so much for searching for Taylor," I say. "Especially after us finding Magdalene the way we did."

Tears crest her swollen eyes and she begins sniffling. "Sorry," she says.

"I was just thinking how everyone is expressing condolences to Keith and Christopher," I say. "Comforting them. You were her mom and—"

"Am," she says. "I *am* her mom. Will always be."

I nod. "Of course. I just meant you had her longer than they did and yet I can't imagine you're receiving even a small portion of the outpouring they are. They are sitting in the parlor getting to grieve and be cared for while you're out here searching for Taylor. I just wanted to let you know that I know they weren't the only ones who lost a child tonight."

She steps toward me and hugs me and starts to cry harder.

"Thank you," she says. "Thank you so much. That means . . . so . . . much. You can't know what that . . . does for me."

We embrace for a long moment.

As we let go of each other she says, "The only other person to express what you are, to check on me in any way—and it really surprised me that she did—was Brooke Wakefield. I'm sure Demi would if she was here. Derinda, if I saw her, but—"

"Demi is here," I say. "She came back to help with the search when she heard what happened."

"*Really?*" she says.

"Yeah. I just saw her a few minutes ago. Why?"

"I'm just surprised," she says. "She was supposed to leave town for a conference earlier tonight. And I'd expect her to call or text me if she was here. You sure it was Demi that you spoke to?"

I nod. "Positive."

"Wow. That's truly . . . strange. I'll have to call or text her to see what's going on. I'm really stunned she hasn't said anything at all—especially given the fact that she knows we found Magdalene. I just thought she didn't know yet."

"Will you do me a favor?" I ask.

"Sure."

"Will you go inside and find Derinda and the boys and let them know how you're feeling?" I say. "Will you give them the chance to console and comfort you even as you try to do it for them?"

She hesitates.

"I can take you in there and explain it to them if you like."

"No, it's not that. I don't mind doing it. I know they'll be great—especially Derinda. She's such a born caregiver . . . and if anyone knows what a mother would be feeling right now . . . but I'd feel guilty taking that much time away from searching for Taylor."

"I understand and appreciate that," I say. "I do, but as Taylor's dad I'm the one asking you to."

She nods and gives me a little smile as more tears stream down her cheeks. "Thank you. Okay, I will. But just for a few minutes."

We begin moving in the direction of the house and Roderick's unmarked.

"You said Brooke had been kind to you," I say. "When and where was that? Do you know where she is now?"

She shakes her head. "That was much earlier. I haven't seen her in a while."

DAY 225

Day 225

All my days aren't total and complete and absolute agony, but most of them are. I have far more bad days than good. Far, far more.

What if I kill myself on one of my particularly bad days, which I have come close to doing many times, and Magdalene comes home a short while later? Right now it's that thought that's keeping me from drinking the Drano in my darkest moments.

41

"Are you sure she doesn't have a kid?" Roderick is asking.

We are standing in what looks like a toddler's room after having searched the rest of the house.

"According to all her friends she doesn't," I say.

"Then this may be one of the creepiest things I've ever seen."

On the drive over we had discussed the legality and morality of breaking into Brooke Wakefield's home if no one was there to let us in, which is what we had expected to be the situation.

After debating whether any judge or jury in the world would consider these exigent circumstances, I concluded that the best thing to do was for me to break in, and, seeing evidence of a break-in, Roderick could enter to investigate.

"Okay," he says, "say she really wants to have a baby or adopt a child, do you do all this before you even have the prospect of having or adopting?"

I think about it.

"What alarms me more than the fact that she would do all

this before having a child is the fact that it looks like a child has stayed in here."

"It does, doesn't it?" he says. "I couldn't figure out what else was bothering me about it, but that's it."

As clean and pristine as the room is, the things in it are not brand-new and unused.

"I suppose it's possible that she bought everything on eBay or at yard sales," I say, "but she doesn't seem like the kind of person who would do that, and nothing else in her house seems secondhand."

"No, it doesn't," he says. "She's always so put together, like she just stepped away from a fashion photoshoot—and her shop and the rest of her house look the same way."

"One possible explanation is that she took Magdalene and kept her in here for a while and then killed her or she died somehow and she placed her body in a freezer. That would explain why she has the room and why it is slightly used."

"If that's the case," he says, "Magdalene's DNA will be in here."

"But if that was the case, Taylor would be in here now," I say.

"Unless she's keeping her somewhere else until the searches are complete."

"But I'm not," Brooke says from the doorway.

We startle and spin around toward her.

"I haven't kidnapped anyone—not Magdalene, not Taylor, no one. I'm not a monster. I'm just a woman without a man who wants a child. Did I jump the gun on creating a nursery? Maybe, but I also use it as my nieces and nephew's room when I keep them." Her eyes lock onto mine. "I understand you're desperate to find your daughter. If I were lucky enough have a child and she went missing I would be too, which is why I'm not going to report you two breaking into my house and violating my privacy and defiling this room that is sacred to me.

That is if you leave right now and don't come back." She turns to Roderick. "And you. Consider yourself in my debt. Just know that if I never need a law enforcement–related favor in the future, it's you I'll be calling."

"I'm sorry," I say. "I was wrong to break in. And you're right it was the act of a desperate person. I'm running out of time and I have no idea where Taylor is. Thanks for being so understanding and please forgive me. But know it's all on me. I did this. Not him. He just came in to make sure I wasn't doing anything else stupid and to take me out."

"He owes me a favor nonetheless," she says. "And I will collect on it one day. Now, if you two are serious about finding that poor little girl, you need to look somewhere else. Because she's not here."

DAY 232

Day 232

How????????????

How the hell was is done?

In addition to everything else—like the who and the why—how Magdalene was even taken is driving me mad.

I can't figure it out.

Even if I'm willing to consider it could be one of our close friends, and at this point I am, I still can't figure out how the hell they did it.

It'd make far, far more sense if it was me or Keith or us working together like so many suspect, but I can't see any way in which someone else could even begin to do it.

It's definitely something I will sit and babble about in my padded room wearing my straitjacket.

42

I'm standing on the empty street in front of Keith and Christopher's home with Henrique Arango at sunrise.

I've spent the night trying to figure out who has Taylor and searching for her—including Clarence and Sarah Samuelson's freezers at The Sand Witch after leaving Brooke Wakefield's house and Wren Melody's bookstore storage room after that.

It's cool and quiet, a slight dampness in the still night air.

A smudge of pale orangish-pink stretches across the eastern horizon like an artist's first stroke on an otherwise untouched canvas.

"Wonder how many more of these I'll see," he says.

That not only makes me mourn for him and for my own mortality, but also question whether Taylor will ever see another one.

"How long do you have?" I ask.

"Minutes, hours, days, weeks maybe," he says. "Probably no longer than that."

"I'm very sorry," I say, and I truly mean it.

"Don't be," he says. "I've gotten far more out of this life than

I ever put in. Sure, I'd like some more time, but I would if I were eighty-six instead of sixty-eight."

I had no idea of his actual age, but even with the ravages of the war he's been fighting visible on the battlefield of his body, I would've said he was younger. He's got a bit of the eternal boy about him, evident in the gleam in his small eyes and the curiosity of a thirst for knowledge still present in his sharp mind.

"As I've gotten closer and closer to my final deadline," he says, "do you know what I've found more and more appealing?"

"What's that?"

"The concept of reincarnation. Do you know how badly I'd like to get another chance at this? I truly believe that given enough attempts, I could finally get this right."

I certainly get the appeal of the great wheel of Samsara, of life and death and rebirth that continues until we've shaken off all the bad karma we've attracted over the years. Who wouldn't want the chance to do it over, better, best?

An intensifying yellow and orange glow along the eastern horizon suddenly bursts into a brilliant translucent gold as the head of the newborn day crowns.

"Welcome," Henrique whispers. "Glad to get to see you."

Nothing in what he's doing is yoga-like in any way, but his greeting of the day causes the words *sun salutation* to come to mind.

He turns toward me suddenly and starts to say something but stops short.

"What?" I ask. "What is it?"

He shakes his head. "Nothing. You didn't come out here to hear the ramblings of a dying old man."

The truth of it is I don't know why I came out here. Except that I'm lost and didn't know what else to do. I wandered out here. I didn't walk out deliberately.

"I just want to get my daughter back," I say. "And I'm not sure how to do that."

"I wish I could tell you," he says. "I really do. I can't imagine the agony you're in. I wonder what's worse—what Keith and Christopher are going through now or what you're going through, what they just went through? Now yours involves most of the agony theirs does, but comes with the added torture of not knowing and the dangerous hope that almost always, inevitably crushes the heart."

"Did you notice anything out of the ordinary last night?" I ask. "Did anyone do anything the least bit suspicious? Or even odd?"

He frowns and shakes his head. "I'm very sorry, but I didn't notice anything like that. Not at all. But the truth is I was probably dozing some of the time. It's not enough that my life will be over too soon to suit me, but I have to miss a lot of the little I have left."

"What about the night that Magdalene was taken?" I say. "Has anything come to mind about that night?"

He shakes his head. "I'm sorry. I've tried and tried to come up with something, but there just isn't anything else."

"What about after that night?" I say. "Did anyone from the group start acting different in the days, weeks, and months following her being taken?"

He shrugs. "Like I've said . . . I just can't . . . I don't remember anything being—anyone being different."

"But you weren't here, were you?" I ask.

"I was here the first few days," he says. "Even took in Keith and Christopher's cat for them, but . . . I left shortly after that."

"How long were you gone?"

"Nearly three months."

"Where were you?" I ask. "What were you doing?"

"I went home," he says. "To Cuba. I found out I was dying

and . . . It was a sort of pilgrimage for me. To the place of my people, of my birth."

"For three months?"

"I also underwent treatment."

"Oh."

"Yeah, as sort of a last . . . hope. A Hail Mary. It was a new, experimental treatment they were trying. Needless to say . . . the experiment failed . . . In my case at any rate."

"I'm very sorry."

He looks back at the sun, sitting just above the tops of the trees in all its bright orange early morning brilliance.

"*No hay mal que por bien no venga*," he says.

I'm not exactly sure what that means, but I think I get the gist of it, and if I'm right, I wonder what good will come out of his death.

"I have seen the sunrise," he says. "Perhaps my last. Now, I must sleep."

He stumbles in the direction of his home a street away and I stumble back toward Keith and Christopher's, far more depleted than I realized.

DAY 237

Day 237

Our committee decided to invite a crime-solving prison chaplain to do our lecture series in the fall, and I'm hoping he will take a look at Magdalene's case for us. Keith has read extensively about him and I heard him interviewed on a few true crime podcasts.

Maybe he will be the very thing we need to stir things up, get things moving again. That seems to be the way of these things—of cold cases. Renewed and intensified interest and or a new investigator causes the criminal to confess or act out in some way—or someone close to them gives them up.

Here's hoping.

43

"We gonna sleep in shifts," Merrill says. "You got the first one. I'll wake you in a few hours."

I shake my head. "I can't."

I have just stumbled wearily into the house and found him looking for me. In addition to telling me that our group—me, him, Dad, Jake, and Reggie—are going to sleep in shifts in a couple of rooms Keith and Christopher have provided for us so some of us can be searching for Taylor around the clock, he has informed me that Roderick has gone home for a few hours of sleep and a shower.

"You can't fall asleep, you can always get back up," he says, "but my money's on the Sand Man."

"I can't stop trying to figure out what happened to Taylor," I say.

"We all gonna keep workin' on that," he says. "Nothin' gonna stop while you do for a few."

"I just can't. Time is running out."

"We all doin' all we can to find her," he says. "We won't stop what we're doin' while you get a little sleep. But unless we just luck up and stumble across her somehow, our best bet of finding her is you figuring out what happened and who did it, and right now the battery in your brain is low. Get a little sleep. Recharge that big brain of yours. It's the very best thing you could do for Taylor."

"If I'm not looking for Taylor, I need to be at the hospital with Anna," I say.

"Anna's being well taken care of," he says. "She'd rather you get some sleep and keep working on finding Taylor and you know it."

"I—"

"But all that's beside the point anyway," he says. "Sorry if I led you to believe I was asking or that your ass had a choice."

"Tell you what," I say, "if you'll drive me to the hospital to check on Anna, I'll sleep in the car on the way there and back."

BUT INSTEAD OF sleeping on the way to the hospital, I open the security footage file on my phone to the exact point I had stopped at the last time I watched it. It's from December 22, the day of the solstice party, and I scan it as we speed down the mostly empty four-lane back road of Highway 98 toward Sacred Heart Hospital in Miramar Beach.

At 2:07 p.m. Hal Raphael exits the front door holding a leather laptop satchel. At 3:11 p.m. Jodi North enters the front door. At 3:39 p.m. Jodi North and Demi Gonzalez exit the front door. At 4:34 p.m. Sarah Samuelson exits the front door. At 4:37 p.m. Hal Raphael enters the front door without his satchel. At 4:40 p.m. Brooke Wakefield exits the front door. At 4:42 p.m. Scott Haskew exits the back door. At 5:37 p.m. Hal Raphael exits the front door. At 5:48 p.m. Keith, Christopher, Magdalene, and Rake Sabin exit the front door. At 7:11 p.m. Christopher, Keith, and Magdalene enter the front door. At 7:37 p.m. Hal Raphael enters the front door. At 7:57 p.m. Brooke Wakefield, Rake Sabin, Wren Melody, Jodi North, Scott Haskew, Henrique

Arango, Sarah and Clarence Samuelson, and Vic Frankford enter the front door—each carrying a Christmas gift.

And then nothing. Just hours and hours of both doors—no one coming or going, entering or exiting from the Florida House.

When the footage ends, I click on the file named 12/23 and continue scanning.

More nothing. More hours of both the front and back doors —and nothing else—until . . .

At 5:43 a.m. Hal Raphael exits the front door rolling a suitcase.

"What's in the suitcase?" I ask.

"Hey," Merrill says. "We're here."

"Huh?"

"We're here."

I open my eyes to see that we are in the parking lot of Sacred Heart.

"How long was I out?" I ask.

"Couple of minutes," he says. "Maybe."

I nod. "Thanks."

He finds a spot not far from the main entrance and parks the car.

"Ready?" I say.

"Sure," he says. "Soon as you tell me what's in the suitcase."

DAY 245

Day 245

    I keep coming back to Raphael. It has to be him. It has to be. I have no idea how he did it exactly, but while we were partying he was doing it. No other explanation makes half as much sense. We need to hire a PI to investigate him, but we're out of money and don't have a heck of a lot coming in. There's got to be a way though. Maybe we could get him back down here somehow.

44

I enter Anna's dim, quiet room to find her sleeping.

She is propped up on pillows and her thick brown hair cascades down around her peaceful, beautiful face.

Verna, who has been asleep in the chair beside Anna's bed, opens her eyes and smiles at me.

"Have y'all found Taylor yet?" she whispers.

"Not yet."

Merrill, who decided not to come in, is grabbing coffee and refueling the car so that we can dash back over right after my brief visit.

"I'm gonna go down and get some breakfast," she says. "Give you two some time alone."

"How has she been?"

"Sleeping mostly."

"Has the doctor been by?"

"Not yet. One saw her in the emergency room. They've run some tests and said a doctor would be by this morning."

"Thank you so much for staying with her," I say.

"My pleasure. I'll be back in a few minutes."

She eases out of the room and pulls the door closed behind her.

I look back at Anna to see if the clicking of the door has awakened her.

Her relaxed and tranquil face looks like an earlier, younger iteration of itself, and I think back to just how long she has been in my life to one degree or another.

I miss her so much—not just the unconscious woman lying in front of me, but my sweet, kind, loving wife who all but vanished a few weeks back.

I've longed for her since she went away, and I've felt isolated and alone.

But as painful and difficult as that has been, I don't think I've ever felt quite as lonely as I do at this moment with Anna asleep, Johanna at her mom's, and Taylor missing.

I feel utterly and completely and absolutely alone.

The ache inside me, the one that permeates my entire being down to the hot lava core of my heart, is not only constant and complete but somehow both dull and acute at the same time.

I want to sit down next to her and cry.

But I know if I do I may not be able to get back up again.

I want to wake her up and seek solace in her.

But I know right now she has none to give and what I would get from her would only make me feel worse.

I want to yell, to rant, to scream, to break and crush and smash something or several somethings, but instead I bow my weary head and beg God to get my wife and daughter back.

A tap at the door is followed by the entrance of a middle-aged Indian man with bushy black hair and a mustache wearing a white lab coat.

"Mr. Jordan?"

I nod and extend my hand.

"I'm Dr. Patel. How are you?"

"Been better."

"Well, hopefully we get your wife better and things get better for you as well. Happy life when wife is happy, no? Have you noticed anxiety, depression, irritability, mood swings?"

I let out a harsh little laugh before I even realize what I'm doing. Nodding perhaps a little too vigorously I say, "A little, yeah."

"Maybe more than little?" he says. "How about fatigue, weight gain, dry skin, joint pain, muscle weakness, stiffness, aches, tenderness? Constipation? Swelling? Trouble sleeping? Irregular menstrual periods?"

I nod. "Some of that for sure. Maybe all of it."

"I want to run a few more tests to confirm, but my guess is the culprit is hypothyroidism. Underactive thyroid disease disorder. It's quite common. Your wife's thyroid gland is not producing enough thyroid hormone. If this assessment is correct, simple treatment with a daily dose of synthetic thyroid hormone and . . . happy life with happy wife."

DAY 250

Day 250

Someone online asked about the possibility that Magdalene's biological mother or father could be responsible. And I was like FUCK I hadn't even thought of that. Of course.

When we asked Roderick Brandt about it he said they had been questioned and that they both had alibis, but he wouldn't tell us who they are. Said he can't.

But anyone can set up a fake alibi, right? I mean, that's exactly what a guilty person does, right?

And here's the kicker . . . by not telling us who they are . . . they could be someone we know—even someone we believe to be a close friend.

45

I walk through the hospital encouraged by Anna's prognosis and return my focus to finding Taylor.

I plan to think about every bit of information I've gathered so far—or at least the ones I can remember—on the drive back to Sandcastle, but I fall asleep in Merrill's passenger seat before we're out of the Sacred Heart parking lot.

Still, my subconscious does the very thing my conscious mind had planned to—and probably far more efficiently.

It comes with a price, however.

My dreams, some of which can only be described as nightmares, are nonsensical, chaotic, and disturbing.

And even one of my recurring dreams is transformed into something it has never been before—something disconcerting, unsettling.

THE LAST OF *the setting sun streaks the blue horizon with neon pink and splatters the emerald green waters of the Gulf with giant orange splotches like scoops of sherbet in an art deco bowl.*

A fitting finale for a perfect Florida day.

Taylor, my daughter, who looks to be around four, though it's hard to tell since in dreams we all seem ageless—runs up from the water's edge, her face red with sun and heat, her hands sticky with wet sand, and asks me to join her for one last swim.

She looks up at me with her mother's brown eyes, open and honest as possible, and smiles her sweetest smile as she begins to beg.

"Please, Daddy," she says. "Please."

"We need to go," I say. "It'll be dark soon. And I'm supposed to take your mom out on a date tonight."

"Please, Daddy," she repeats as if I have not spoken, and now she takes the edge of my swimming trunks in her tiny, sandy hand and tugs.

I look down at her, moved by her openness, purity, and beauty.

She knows she's got me then.

"Yes," she says, releasing my shorts to clench her fist and pull it toward her in a gesture of victory. Then she begins to jump up and down.

I drop the keys and the towels and the bottles of sunscreen wrapped in them, kick off my flip-flops, and pause just a moment to take it all in—her, the sand, the sea, the sun.

"I love you, Dad," she says with the ease and unashamed openness only a safe and secure child can.

"I love you."

I take her hand in mine, and we walk down to the end of her world as the sun sets and the breeze cools off the day.

I look down and she is gone, her tiny, sandy hand no longer in my own.

I spin around and look for her, searching in every direction.

In the far distance I see a small figure that might be her.

I race toward her.

But no matter how hard or fast I run I can't gain any ground, can't make up any of the distance between us.

And then she is gone.

Suddenly the beach breeze brings with it shrieks and cries, and I can't determine if they are hers or the gulls gliding in the air over sea and shore.

I WAKE GROGGILY and discombobulated as my phone vibrates incessantly in my pocket.

I withdraw it and squint to read the name on the display.

It's Roderick.

"Just got a call from the ME," he says. "Prelim autopsy shows no signs of sexual assault or violence."

"Thank God for that," I say, thinking not only of Magdalene but where Taylor might be right now and what might be being done to her.

"The body had been frozen shortly after death just as we had suspected," he says. "And she estimates the body, which has been cleaned, had been out of the freezer less than sixteen hours or so."

I'm doing my best to focus on what he's saying and to add it to the other information that I've acquired so far, but my mind keeps trying to break in with the thought that I already know who did it.

"But the biggest revelation came from the rushed drug screenings," he says. "Like so many in the media and online have theorized, she did die of a drug overdose—and it was sleeping medication. Something called chloral hydrate. Evidently it's pretty common."

I sit for a long moment taking it all in, adding it to everything else I know, and allowing the thought that I already know who did it to fully form within my conscious mind.

"You there?" he says eventually.

"I think I know who did it," I say. "You mind if I try something unconventional?"

46

We enter the front door of the Florida House the way they did for the solstice party last year—en masse.

Wren Melody, Brooke Wakefield, Henrique Arango, Scott Haskew, Clarence and Sarah Samuelson, Jodi North, Vic Frankford, Rake Sabin, Hal Raphael, Roderick Brandt, Dad, Jake, Reggie, and me.

Making our way into the parlor, we join Keith, Derinda, Charis, and Christopher, who are all sitting on the same couch beside each other dozing.

They stir awake and sit up as we enter.

I had asked Roderick if we could gather together everyone who was in the house the night of the solstice and he had said he was willing to try anything.

Everyone is obviously exhausted—disheveled and drowsy.

"Could we have everyone who was at the party the night Magdalene was taken sit down in the parlor?" Roderick says.

Keith and Christopher remain where they are, as Scott and Vic replace Derinda and Charis on the couch with them.

Wren and Brooke sit on the loveseat.

Henrique takes the chair by the fireplace.

Rake sits in a high-back chair near another couch where Clarence and Sarah Samuelson are seated with Jodi North.

Everyone else is either in the doorway of the foyer area or dining room—Dad, Derinda, Charis and Reggie on the dining room side and Roderick, Jake, and Raphael in the opening to the foyer.

"Not just at the party that night," I say, looking at Raphael, "but in the house. Would you join the others in here?"

He shakes his head, frowns, stomps into the parlor, and takes the last remaining empty chair—an uncomfortable-looking upright wooden one.

"We'll bring around some coffee," Derinda says, and she and Charis busy themselves doing just that.

"Thank you," I say.

Roderick takes a step forward and says, "John has some things to say and some questions to ask. I want everyone to give him your undivided attention and unreserved cooperation."

Merrill is the only one not present, and that's because I have him checking on something for me that might verify and validate the theory I've formulated.

Because I have to buy some time while waiting to find out what he uncovers, and because it will help me further solidify and bolster or discredit and abandon my theory, I have decided to talk through what I'm thinking with the suspects.

I feel more like Hercule Poirot than I ever imagined I could and I have the urge to say *Madame* and *Monsieur*.

I resist the urge.

"Until last night," I say, "we didn't know who took Magdalene, how it was done, or if she was still alive or not. Until a few minutes ago we didn't know how she was killed, how her body was put back in her bed, and who took Taylor from our bedroom."

"You saying you know now?" Keith says.

I nod.

"How Magdalene was killed or all of it?" he says.

"*Why* is what I want to know," Christopher says. "Why would anyone steal our little angel?"

"Let's talk through all of it," I say, pulling out my phone to make sure I haven't missed a message from Merrill. "We can start with the security system here. No one can enter without having a current key card or being let in. And anyone who does enter or exit is recorded by the security cameras. It's because of them that we know no one entered the house after you guys arrived for the party. And no one left until Hal Raphael left for the airport the following morning. But he appeared to be alone."

"I didn't *appear* to be alone," he says. "I *was* alone."

"There was no sign of Magdalene when the rest of you came out of the house to look for her later that morning," I say. "So if no one breaks into the house after the party starts, then it has to be one of you already in the house. But even as we're able to narrow it down to you all, that doesn't tell us how you did what you did with all the other people in the house or how you were able to remove Magdalene from the house without being seen."

"Does it have something to do with the key card that was stolen that day?" Christopher asks.

"The truth is . . . I'm not sure."

"What?" Vic says. "You either know or you don't. I thought you corralled us all in here like cattle because you knew."

"I do believe the killer stole the key card," I say. "I just don't know if it was used in the commission of the crime. What I mean is . . . the killer could've used it but didn't necessarily have to in order to get in or out of the house. I'm still left with some questions about the key cards—including my own. When I was trying to get back into our room to see if the secret passageway was used to take Taylor mine didn't work, but instead of it having something to do with the crime, I may have just been rushing too much and didn't give it enough time to work. I don't know for sure. What I *am* sure of is that the key card that was stolen wouldn't have to have been used for the crime to have been committed."

"It seems like you're dragging this out just to torture us," Brooke says.

"Yeah," Clarence says. "Why don't you tell us what you know instead of what you don't know?"

I glance at my phone again as Derinda and Charis begin passing out the coffee.

"What we now know for sure," I say, "is that Magdalene died of a sleeping aid overdose. The drug screening the lab ran this morning reveals that."

"Just like the media reported," Vic says. "So . . . it was an accidental death."

Everyone looks over at Keith and Christopher.

"Look over here all you want," Keith says. "We didn't give her any goddamn sleeping medication that night."

"We certainly didn't," Christopher says.

"Yes, you did," I say. "You both did."

"I swear to God we didn't," Keith says. "Swear on . . . on . . . my life. What there is left of it."

"You did," I say again. "You both did. And Magdalene wasn't the only one drugged that night. You all were. Everyone but the killer was. That's how this was done. Recall how everyone of you told me what an off year it was, how exhausted everyone was, how normally everyone stays up late and some of you stay up all night, but this year most of you didn't even make it up to your room, you slept in here—on the couch, the chair, the floor, propped up on the dining room table. It's because you were all drugged."

"How?" Wren Melody asks. "Tell us how, dear boy?"

"The solstice punch," I say. "Both versions—the virgin and

the alcoholic so that everyone would be. And before putting Magdalene to bed . . ."

"We let her have some of the virgin punch," Keith says.

"Oh, my God," Christopher says. "We killed her."

Derinda quickly hands Charis the coffee she's holding and rushes over to comfort her boys.

"I don't think so," I say. "I don't think it was enough to kill her. I think the killer gave her sleeping medication later not knowing she already had some in her system from the punch. They just thought she was groggy from having been asleep, so they gave her the meds they had intended to all along—and together it was too much."

"So," Henrique says, "that means her death was accidental."

I nod. "I believe so. I believe this was an abduction gone wrong."

I pause for a moment and check my phone again as everyone digests what has been said so far.

"So," I say. "Who did it? Why did they do it? And how did they get Magdalene's body out of the house and then back in it nearly a year later—or did they? Was it in here all along? Let's start with motive. Why would someone abduct a child?" I look at Brooke. "Perhaps because she wants her for her own. Or," I add, looking at Raphael, "perhaps for far more sinister reasons. Or maybe," I say, glancing back at Henrique, "it was so she could be traded on a black market barter system in an attempt to get experimental medical treatment."

Vic looks at me and shakes his head, then over to Roderick, "If y'all drag this out any longer I'm gonna confess just to get it over with."

"We'll come back to motive in a minute," I say. "Let's talk about how Magdalene's body could've been removed from the house without being noticed. If we go just by the security footage, then the most obvious way is in Hal Raphael's suitcase that he left with the following morning. It was big enough."

"I didn't kill that little girl," Raphael says. "Accidentally or otherwise, and I didn't put her body in my suitcase and carry it out of here."

My phone vibrates and I pull it out. It's a text from Merrill.

You were right. Her body was definitely in the freezer here.

"Okay," I say, "let's say you didn't. If that's not how Magdalene was removed from the house, then how was she? Because the security footage doesn't show another way it could've been done. But . . . what the security footage does show is how the abductor become killer entered the house. And it was right through the front door."

"You've already said that," Sarah Samuelson says.

"It just wasn't when it appeared to be," I say. "It wasn't when you all came back for the party but earlier in the day—a good deal earlier. The security footage shows everyone entering the house and later leaving except for one person. One person entered the house and didn't leave—never left again according to the footage." I turn to Charis Tremblay. "The video shows you coming in like so many others that day, carrying Christmas presents, which are still unopened in Magdalene's room. But it doesn't show you leave. It has been right there all along but must have been overlooked during the first investigation."

She freezes in the doorway between the dining room and parlor, a pitcher of coffee dangling from her hand.

Everyone turns toward her.

"You snatched the key card at some point—though I'm not sure you ever used it—and when no one noticed, you found a place to hide. You hid until everyone left for the candlelight service, and while they were there, you made your preparations and put the sleep meds in the punch and then went and hid in Magdalene's room. You were her mother and you just couldn't abide the thought of two men—two gay men—raising your little girl. So you were just going to put everyone to sleep, including her, and take her back. Only when you gave her a dose of sleep aid there was already a good bit in her little body, which meant you killed the very little girl you were, in your mind, trying to protect."

"Oh *God*," Christopher says. "Is it true? Did you pretend to accept us just so you could steal our—"

"*My*," she says. "She was *my* daughter, not yours. A little girl needs a mother, not two sodomites."

"I will kill you with my bare hands," Keith says, rising from the couch.

Jake steps between him and Charis as Roderick walks over and puts a hand on Keith's shoulder and gently pushes him back down on the couch.

"I didn't mean to hurt her," she says. "It was an accident. I would gladly trade places with her. I would never do anything to harm her. I loved that child. Loved her in a way only a godly mother can. I've grieved for her every single day since y'all took her from me—doubly since she died."

"Not since she died—since *you killed her*," Christopher says.

"You evil bitch," Keith says. "What the fuck was organizing the searches in the woods about? Pretending to care about us and help us?"

"It was all to deflect suspicion," I say, "and to bide her time until she could frame you two for Magdalene's death. I think she figured out what happened and froze the body so she could eventually use it to set you guys up. My guess is she was the source close to the investigation who started the rumor about you two accidentally overdosing her. She figured if she froze the body, spread that rumor, then eventually put her back in your house it'd look like you really did it."

"It wasn't enough to take her from us, you had to set us up for killing her?"

"*You* took her from *me*," she says, her voice rising. "She'd still be alive if you hadn't taken her away from me. God is punishing you for your abominations."

"The whole time you're out there searching for her in those woods with the rest of us," Derinda says, "you knew she was dead, knew we wouldn't find anything."

"As recently as last night, even after she had snuck Magdalene's dead body back into her bed," I say, "she was telling me how if we found Magdalene alive she was going to try to get custody back."

"A liar until the very end," Keith says. "A thief, a murderer, a liar. How can you break like every one of the commandments and still believe you're the good guy and we're the bad guys?"

"Because she's certifiable," Christopher says. "Fuckin' nuts."

"But," Henrique says, "how did she leave the house with Magdalene without being seen that night?"

"While you were all passed out," I say. "And the security cameras didn't capture her because she went through the pet door on the side of the house—she and Magdalene were about the only ones small enough to fit through it."

"How did she get the body back in the house?" Rake asks.

"And what was that business with the pajamas?" Vic asks.

"The pajamas were a distraction," I say. "And while everyone was over at the search site trying to see what was going on, she came back here, supposedly to make tea and coffee for everyone, but it was really to return Magdalene to her bed. My guess is that she brought the body back into the house inside of a box or suitcase—just walked right in the front door with her while everyone else was over at the search site. We'll have to check the security camera footage to be sure, but she got her body back into the house without being observed. And I knew when I saw the care with which Magdalene had been treated—the bathing and cleaning—that it had to be done by someone who not only knew her but loved her. And the white gown and headband and candles was so ritualistic that I thought it was likely to have been done by a religious person."

"I loved that little girl more than any of you can imagine," she says. "I'm not a—I just did what any good mother would do."

"How much was your husband involved?" I ask.

She lets out a harsh laugh. "Brent's as clueless as the rest of y'all. Always traveling. This past year do you know how many days a month he's been home on average? Three. Three days a month. And when he is . . . he never pays any mind to me or my kids. That's what he calls my foster children. *My* kids. I knew he would never even come into my little craft shed let alone look in the freezer, but I kept a lock on it anyway. Buying that lock was a waste of money. He's the most incurious man you ever met—especially about his wife and what she gets up to. He helped with the grid for the search and showed up a time or two, but Magdalene was never his and his heart was never in it."

My phone vibrates again. I pull it out and see I have another text from Merrill.

She's not here. I've searched the entire house and property.

"Where is she?" I ask Charis.

She looks confused. "Who?"

"Taylor," I say. "Where is Taylor?"

She shakes her head and shrugs. "I have no idea. I'm not a kidnapper, not some sort of monster who steals children. I was a desperate mother trying to get her daughter back from these filthy faggots. I didn't take your child. I had no reason to. And think about it—I was with you when it happened."

She's right and I know it. I can tell she's telling the truth.

"I'll take a lie detector test," she says. "But I'm telling you I didn't take your daughter. I wouldn't. And I'm telling you for two reasons . . . I want you to keep looking for her because I don't have her. And because of the way all y'all are looking at me. I feel all your judgement and disdain, but think about this . . . if I didn't take her that means one of y'all did."

47

"She could be lying," Roderick says.

I shake my head. "She's not."

I'm in shock, can feel myself going numb, part of me growing distant from other parts of me.

I keep shaking my head in stunned wonder. "What did I miss? How did I not see that she had only taken Magdalene?"

Roderick, Reggie, Merrill, Dad, Jake, and I are standing in the dining room. A deputy has just taken Charis away in hand-cuffs and the others—apart from Keith, Christopher, and Derinda—have disassembled and wandered off, some to sleep, others to resume searching for the daughter I thought I had found.

"The most important case of my life and I blew it," I say.

"We gonna find her," Merrill says. "We just need to regroup. Keep searching. Keep investigating."

They all nod.

Dad says, "He's right. We just get back out there and keep knocking on doors, keep looking, keep following up leads. Simple shoe leather. Good old-fashioned police work. We will find her, Son."

"We've got to look at everyone again," Roderick says. "Our prime suspects have to be Rake Sabin and Hal Raphael."

Reggie nods.

"I . . . can't believe I . . . just missed completely that it could be two different criminals. I'm . . . It was a rookie mistake."

"Listen," Jake says, "you just got justice for that family in there. They went from knowing nothing to knowing everything thanks to you—and the bitch who did it is in jail. Now we'll do the same thing for Taylor."

"I don't want justice," I say. "I want her back."

"That's what I meant," he says. "You know I ain't no good at this shit. All I'm sayin' is don't give up. We got this. We're all gonna help you and we're gonna find her."

"I wish y'all'd stop saying that," I say. "Every time you do it makes it more certain that we won't."

DAY 328

Day 328

I thought knowing would make things better. And I guess it does take away some of the anxiety that not knowing brings—some of the torment your imagination subjects you to—but it also crushes even the smallest fragments of hope.

Whatever percentage of dread and anxiety and hope I had has now been replaced by overwhelming, unabating agony.

Sadness is all now. Unforgiving, unrelenting anguish.

My little girl is gone and she's never coming back to me.

48

Days go by.

We continue to search.

We continue to investigate.

I go through everything over and over again, frantically searching for what I missed.

I run through every scenario I can come up with, search every possible location I can conceive of.

But ultimately nothing we try does any good.

Taylor is gone.

I failed to protect her.

I'm failing to find her.

The only feeling that comes anywhere close to the devastating pain and emptiness I feel is the overwhelming and near debilitating guilt.

This is my fault. I am responsible. I put Taylor in this situation. I didn't keep her safe. And now I am unable to find her, unable to figure out who took her and how, unable to get her and return her safely home.

I now know what so many people I've worked with over the years have known—just how excruciating the pain is, just how huge a hole it leaves in your soul, just how relentless the torment of not knowing is.

I feel absolutely numb and in acute agony all the time.

I am frustrated and agitated, irritable and overly sensitive, in many ways a stranger to myself.

All my experience as an investigator, all my study and research, all my decades of practice going back to adolescence —everything I have used over and over for others in crisis I am unable to use for my child, my wife, myself.

Physician heal thyself. He saved others, himself he cannot save.

I feel like a fraud.

I feel like a failure.

I'm experiencing feelings of impotency and uselessness that I could never have even imagined before now.

And yet I don't care how I feel. I'd gladly live in this total torment for the rest of my life if we could just get Taylor back.

It's all I care about. It's all that matters. It's everything—and the one thing I am unable to do anything about.

49

On the eighth day of Taylor being missing, I arrive home late from investigating and searching in Sandcastle to find Anna packing.

It's in no way surprising, not in the least unexpected, but the blow is still staggering.

Unable to speak, I sit on the bed that until a few weeks ago I thought would always be ours, and try my best not to cry or put my hand through the wall.

Anna is looking down as she goes about her tasks, but as her hair moves I can see that she is quietly crying.

"I . . . I'm not sure what to say," she says. "I just need to be alone right now. Everything's murky right now, but . . . this has more to do with grief than anger, more about me than you."

I have no words, no outward response except a sad little nod.

"I'm sorry for how I treated you when my thyroid was . . . wasn't working properly. I'll regret that the rest of my life."

I shake my head and try to wave her apology off, but she isn't looking at me.

Though the chainsaws and generators can no longer be

heard through the night, the increased truck traffic and night crews working around town still can be, and I think about how my hurricane-ravaged region looks like I feel.

"I know this doesn't matter," she says. "Nothing does, does it? But I'm not leaving to punish you. I'm really not. If I could stay I would."

I nod but she doesn't see it.

"I need to be alone right now," she says. "Have to be. In many ways I already have been, but I . . . I just can't be here—not in this house, not in this life . . . or whatever it is."

With all we've been through we've never known brokenness like this before. And to be experiencing it at the same time, each unable to help the other . . . is a hopelessness like none other I've ever known.

"I'm sorry," I say. "I'm so sorry."

I bite the inside of my cheek to keep from breaking down and I can taste the blood in my mouth.

"I should've never taken us over there," I say. "And the moment I had even an inkling that it might not be safe I should have grabbed y'all and left."

"I . . . I wasn't going to say anything," she says. "It doesn't help and . . . But . . . I am going to say this and then I won't ever say it or anything else about this ever again."

I brace myself for what she's about to say, though I have no idea what it is.

"The night . . . the night she was taken . . . you wanted us to leave then . . . before it happened. And I realize I'm the one who said we could protect her until the next morning and leave then, but . . . you knew something was wrong with me. You could tell by my behavior that I was . . . unwell . . . irrational . . . incapable of making reasoned decisions . . . So why did you let me decide? Why didn't . . . when I needed you to most . . . why didn't you make the right decision for us, for our family, for your child?"

50

The late-evening sun is low and soft, its deep red rays like blood on the beach.

Following a particularly difficult day of searching for Taylor and investigating what happened to her, I'm standing barefooted before the gentle green tide of the Gulf in nearly the exact spot Taylor and I had the day we first arrived at Sandcastle for my lecture series and our vacation.

It has been two weeks since Taylor was taken, and I'm no closer to finding her now than when she first vanished.

On either side of me the beach is mostly empty—only the occasional lone sun-tinged figure in the distance—as is much of the town of Sandcastle behind me.

I think about what a solitary sun-tinged figure I am.

Over the course of a lifetime of loneliness, I've never felt more isolated, more utterly and completely alone.

I tried bringing Johanna here on one of our recent days together—my fear and paranoia wouldn't let me take her into town—but like most of the times I'm with her these days, I couldn't stop crying and holding and hugging her.

I am haunted by Anna's final words to me, that I am ultimately responsible for Taylor's abduction, that not preventing it when Anna was essentially incapacitated rests squarely on my bent shoulders.

I am even more haunted by how every cell that makes up me is in complete agreement with her.

I am tormented every second of every day—both waking and sleeping—wondering and worrying about where Taylor is and what horrific experiences she could be going through.

The acute affliction of my anguish is incessant, and I feel as though I'm losing the moorings of my mind.

The insidiousness of this particular torture is that the very thing I need to find her—my mind—is under continuous assault.

Despite all this, I will not stop, *cannot* stop my search, my relentless pursuit of her.

The only respite of any kind at all that I get these days is coming here—to this place where she and I had kicked off our shoes and enjoyed the morning sun-warmed sand together.

I feel her here, her sweet, kind, carefree presence, and I am buoyed up by it—at least to the extent that I can be.

At a time when I have little to hold on to, little to be thankful for, I'm so, so glad I brought her here when she asked me to, when I was only minutes away from giving my first talk and could have used those same minutes in final preparations.

We shared a moment here that, though everything else has been taken from me, remains fixed and firm in my wounded heart and embattled mind.

And as the last of the setting sun sinks into the green-gold Gulf, I say to her what I always say to her before leaving this now sacred spot.

"I *will* find you," I whisper. "I swear it."

51

I walk back to my car thinking about mothers—and in my isolation and desperation, missing my own.

I think about Charis and how she truly believed she was Magdalene's mother, how what she did, as misguided and ultimately evil as it was, was understandable. I could understand a mother like her far more than one like Magdalene's biological mother who could give her up and not want anything to do with her.

And then I think of Anna.

All thoughts about motherhood and everything else these days lead me back to Anna and Taylor.

I yearn for Anna, long to have Taylor back, so deeply and desperately I feel as if I might collapse from the weight of it.

Eventually, my thoughts lead me to Susan, the mother of my oldest daughter, Johanna. I think about the mother that she is, and how regardless of how fraught our relationship can be, I never question her love for and devotion to our daughter.

I think about how often she has questioned the care I give my daughters—not just the one we share together, but both of them—specifically when it comes to their safety. She has voiced her concern on several occasions—especially while we were dealing with the erratic, volatile, and violent behavior of Anna's ex, Chris Taunton, and after what happened during Hurricane Michael some six weeks ago.

I think about how she has kept Johanna from me at times, and how cagey she's been lately, and a thought flashes into my mind—what if she took Taylor? What if she did it for Taylor—out of concern for her? For Johanna—so she could have her little sister with her all the time? For herself—as a mother wanting control, as an ex wanting revenge?

And then I know. I know who has my daughter and I know why.

And I race to my car to go get her.

52

"I should've seen it sooner," I say.

I'm back at the Florida House.

Keith, Christopher, and I are once again sitting at their kitchen table in their residence, while Sarah Samuelson, Brooke Wakefield, and Wren Melody hang Christmas decorations in the main hallway and parlor and Derinda cleans upstairs.

On my way over I called Merrill, Anna, and Roderick, and asked for their help.

"In both cases this was about mothers doing what they thought was best for their children," I say. "Charis stole Magdalene out of a misguided sense of motherhood and Derinda stole Taylor for that same reason."

I carefully watch and weigh their reactions.

Keith begins shaking his head immediately, his shock obvious, but behind his instant denial there is definite doubt in his hard, squinting eyes.

Christopher's mouth drops open and he looks surprised but not stunned.

Their responses seem authentic.

"She has been watching how heartbroken you guys are for so long," I say, "and she just wanted to help, to soothe the ache in your soul, to ease your pain even if only a little by replacing Magdalene with Taylor. Taylor is about the age Magdalene would have been if she had lived. Derinda's the only one who could've done it besides you two and that's part of why I'm here —to find out if you had anything to do with it."

Christopher says, "We could never . . . never do to someone else what was done to us."

"I'm not convinced she did it," Keith says, "but if she did, we're not involved in any way."

"Has she told you what she did?" I ask. "Has she tried to give Taylor to you yet or is she still waiting for all the attention to die down?"

"I don't believe she could do something like that," Keith says. "I really don't."

"I bet she didn't either," I say, "right up until she did it."

"I know you were right about Charis," he says, "but I think you're way off on this."

"How?" Christopher asks. "How'd she do it?"

"She cleans the house for you," I say. "She knows it intimately. She used the secret passageway in order to get from back here in your residence to our room. She snuck in through the fireplace, took Taylor and brought her back down here to your residence. She took quite a chance, but got lucky that Anna was sick and she and Taylor are deep sleepers. Or, who knows, maybe she found a way to slip them something earlier in the evening. While she was cleaning earlier, she unlocked the fireplace so she could get in. After she had taken her, she gave Taylor something to make sure she stayed asleep and hid her little body in the cleaning cart beneath the sheets and towels. She did this as I was talking to Charis on the landing.

She went to the parlor and sat with everyone for a while. And at some point, probably while everyone was focused on Raphael, she slipped behind the desk and disabled the cameras. She then she walked out the front door with Henrique, creating the perfect alibi. Maybe she even drove off a short distance, but as soon as she saw that Henrique had gone inside his house, she circled back, went in through the back door, removed Taylor from the cleaning cart, and snuck her out. When she had finished cleaning earlier, she put the cart in the storage closet, but when we were searching for Taylor later, the cleaning cart was out in the hallway. I think that was from when she rushed in and grabbed Taylor out of it. Remember, Keith, you actually put it back in the closet after we searched it. She was able to get Taylor out of the area and back to her house and hidden before the roadblocks were in place. When you called her she came right back to further establish her alibi and act as if she had nothing to do with it. We've been searching Sandcastle and she's even helped us because it didn't matter. Taylor was long gone—outside of Sandcastle before we ever started looking for her here. What I want to know is did you know?"

"No," Keith says.

"Did you have anything to do with it?"

"Absolutely not."

"Has she told you about it? About doing it?"

Keith shakes his head.

Christopher says, "Now that I'm thinking about it . . . she may have hinted at it. I didn't think anything of it at the time, but . . . I don't know . . . She may have hinted to me about us getting another daughter at some point."

"I'm going to talk to her before I do anything else," I say. "Do you guys want to be present for that? And if you are, will you help and not hinder?"

"If she did do it," Keith says, "what are you going to do to her?"

"I'm not going to do anything," I say. "I only care about getting Taylor back. If she's helpful with that it will go a long way for her with whatever the Walton County Sheriff's Department decides to do."

53

"Oh my God, what have I done?" Derinda says, tears streaming down her cheeks in what appears to be genuine remorse.

She is now at the kitchen table with us, having just confirmed much of what I had come to believe about what happened.

"So, it's true?" Keith says. "Mama, are you . . . You really did it?"

"John," she says, "I'm so sorry. I just went a little mad. I've never believed in temporary insanity before, but . . . I don't know what I've been thinking." She turns to Keith and Christopher. "I've just watched you boys suffer so much for so long and then after all that time . . . to find her . . . dead."

"You took Taylor *before* Magdalene's body was discovered," I say.

"I just thought, I've got to do something to stop the pain," she continues, ignoring what I've just said. "I've got to help them. They are my boys, my sons. But I knew I was wrong even as I was doing it—and especially after I did it, but then . . . I wasn't sure how to undo it. So I just kept doing it, trying to figure out a way to either tell Keith and Christopher eventually or to somehow return Taylor to you and Anna. I'm so sorry. I can't tell you how relieved I am that you know."

"Is she alive?" I ask. "Is she okay? Where is she?"

"I have treated that little girl like a princess," she says. "I have taken such good care of her. She has been safe and loved and doted on. She just thinks that I'm keeping her for you guys while you help Keith and Christopher find their little girl."

"Where is she?" I ask.

"My house."

"Who keeps her while you come here?"

"I leave her at home."

"Who is with her right now?" I ask. "Because Merrill, Anna, and Roderick are about to enter your house to get her and I want to know who's in there with her."

"No one," she says. "I just give her a little sleeping medicine and I never stay gone for very long."

"Mom," Keith says.

"I leave cartoons playing in her bedroom and lock the door in case she wakes up."

"Are you hearing yourself?" Keith says. "Listen to what you're saying."

"But she never has woken up and I always get back very quickly. I'm so sorry. I can't believe I did this. I'm still shocked at my own actions—especially hearing it out loud like this now. It was like something just came over me. I'm not someone who would do something like this."

"But you are," Keith says. "Turns out you're exactly someone who would do something like this."

"*Keith*," she says, as if he has slapped her hard across the face.

"You better hope to God she's okay," he says. "Because if she's not . . ."

"She is. I swear it."

54

"I think I'm almost out of hugs," Taylor is saying.

Anna and I both laugh, but she doesn't look at me like she once would have.

"We've just missed you so much," I say. "Sorry if we're making you sore from all the hugs."

"It's okay. I missed y'all too."

The three of us are in a booth inside the Donut Hole on 98.

We're actually on the same side of the booth. Though the other side of the booth is empty, neither of us wants to be that far from her just now.

In addition to over-hugging her, we're allowing Taylor to have as many doughnuts and as much ice cream as she wants.

"Did you find Mr. Keith and Mr. Christopher's little girl?" she asks.

"We did," I say.

"That's good," she says. "Makes it worth it then I guess."

I shake my head. "No, it doesn't. Sorry, but it just doesn't. I missed you way, way too much. I don't ever want to be apart again, okay?"

"Okay, Daddy."

So far we haven't gotten into the real reason she was kept away from us for two weeks. It is only one of so many things that are still open and unresolved, like wounds that have yet to heal.

But in the light of having her alive, having her safely back, not much else seems to matter.

Like me, most of Anna's attention has been directed toward Taylor. I have no idea what she's thinking or how she's feeling —especially about us and our future. She certainly hasn't given me any indication that getting Taylor back makes her want to get back with me. But even that—as much as that matters, as vital that is—even it dims in the brilliant light of having our daughter back and our need to celebrate her return.

For this my daughter was dead, and is alive again; she was lost, and is found. And they began to be merry.

I think about how many cases I've worked over the years where children weren't found alive, didn't get to come home, weren't able to be hugged too much and have doughnuts and ice cream. Even as I grieve for Martin Fisher, Nicole Caldwell, Mariah Evers, Magdalene Dacosta, and the one who haunts me the most, Derek Burrell, I rejoice all the more that Taylor isn't among them, that for once the disappeared has reappeared, that the lost has been found, that my daughter who was dead is alive again.

GET A JOHN JORDAN CHRISTMAS NOW

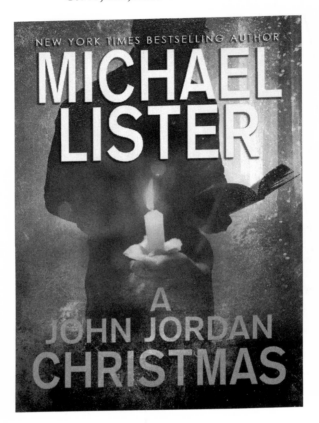

ALSO BY MICHAEL LISTER

Books by Michael Lister

(John Jordan Novels)

Power in the Blood

Blood of the Lamb

Flesh and Blood

(Special Introduction by Margaret Coel)

The Body and the Blood

Double Exposure

Blood Sacrifice

Rivers to Blood

Burnt Offerings

Innocent Blood

(Special Introduction by Michael Connelly)

Separation Anxiety

Blood Money

Blood Moon

Thunder Beach

Blood Cries

A Certain Retribution

Blood Oath

Blood Work

Cold Blood

Blood Betrayal

Blood Shot

Blood Ties

Blood Stone

Blood Trail

Bloodshed

Blue Blood

And the Sea Became Blood

The Blood-Dimmed Tide

Blood and Sand

A John Jordan Christmas

(Jimmy Riley Novels)

The Girl Who Said Goodbye

The Girl in the Grave

The Girl at the End of the Long Dark Night

The Girl Who Cried Blood Tears

The Girl Who Blew Up the World

(Merrick McKnight / Reggie Summers Novels)

Thunder Beach

A Certain Retribution

Blood Oath

Blood Shot

(Remington James Novels)

Double Exposure

(includes intro by Michael Connelly)

Separation Anxiety

Blood Shot

(Sam Michaels / Daniel Davis Novels)

Burnt Offerings

Blood Oath

Cold Blood

Blood Shot

(Love Stories)

Carrie's Gift

(Short Story Collections)

North Florida Noir

Florida Heat Wave

Delta Blues

Another Quiet Night in Desperation

(The Meaning Series)

Meaning Every Moment

The Meaning of Life in Movies

Made in the USA
Coppell, TX
07 February 2020

15584742R00173